Valentine Delights

Valentine Delights

From the Editors
Of *True Story* And
True Confessions

Published by True Renditions, LLC

True Renditions, LLC
105 E. 34th Street, Suite 141
New York, NY 10016

Copyright @ 2013 by True Renditions, LLC

ISBN: 978-1-938877-94-0

Visit us on the web at www.truerenditionsllc.com.

Contents

THE VALENTINE'S DAY CURSE

Gran's sharp words caught me by surprise. "Valerie, you can't get married on Valentine's Day!"

I thought she would be delighted with my good news. She knew Sterling, and said he was a "fine young man." He and I had been to her place several times during the past weeks—and they both seemed to take a real liking to each other. I took it for granted that she would welcome him into our family with open arms.

"Why can't we get married on Valentine's Day, Gran?" I questioned as I sat on the sofa in her living room. "You know Sterling. I thought you liked him. I know he thinks a lot of you, Gran. He tells me you are the grandmother he never had. To him, you are special."

She sat in her recliner, her thin hands moving anxiously in her lap. How many times had I seen those same gentle hands reach out to touch and soothe my fevered forehead or tie a ribbon in my hair? How many times had those hands worked diligently knitting sweaters and Afghans and gloves, which she gave freely to those who were dear to her? Now the arthritis in her hands prevented her from doing so many of the things she loved to do.

As I looked at her hands now and saw them moving nervously, I knew she was really upset with me. The very fact that I had upset her was upsetting to me. Yet, I couldn't understand why my marrying Sterling Billingsley would cause her distress.

"No, you cannot do it!" she insisted. "It will never last!" Her words almost had a touch of fear in them.

"Gran, what's wrong?" I asked. "Sterling is a good man. You know him. You know he is good and kind and gentle. He loves me. I love him. He and I . . ."

She nodded in agreement. "Yes, that's true, he is all those things. And yes, he would be a wonderful husband for you, Valerie. And you should marry him. But not on Valentine's Day!"

I shook my head. None of this made any sense. "Why not?" I asked.

"Haven't you ever heard the old saying 'If you marry on Valentine's Day your love is sure to fade away'? It's the Valentine's Day Curse! You cannot marry Sterling on Valentine's Day. It's bad luck. Your marriage will never last."

I looked over at Gran and smiled. There she goes again, I thought. Gran and her old sayings.

For as long as I could recall, Gran had been a steadying force in my life. When Mom and Dad divorced, I was sent to live with Gran. I was only eight years old at the time. She lived alone in her small house on the other side of town. Mom had seldom taken me to visit her own mother, so when I moved in with Gran, she and I were strangers. But I was Gran's daughter's child, so Gran welcomed me with open arms and an open heart.

As I look back on it, I'm sure there were times I was difficult for her—I was an active child, running and playing and climbing the apple tree in her back yard. I roller skated with Jenny, the girl next door; I played ball with other neighborhood kids and came home with scratches and cuts on my knees or elbows. Gran never scolded me—she just bandaged the wound, gave me a hug and sent me back out to play.

Gran was always my strongest supporter. There was a special bond between us. She encouraged me to try things—piano lessons, dance lessons, painting, rock collecting. "The more you try, the more you learn," she told me whenever I came up with a new "project" such a baton twirling or swimming classes or collecting golden leaves in the autumn.

That saying was like so many of her other ones. She seemed to have one for every occasion. And she believed each and every one of them. She was always telling me, "Red sky in the morning--sailor take warning!" Or she would say, "If you drop a fork on the floor it is a sure sign that a man will come to your door; if you drop a spoon on the floor, then a woman will come to your door."

I recall her telling me, "If your left hand itches, you are getting money; if your right hand itches, you will meet someone new."

Sometimes when Jenny and I got to giggling and acting silly she would caution, "The harder you laugh, the harder you will cry."

No matter what the situation was, she had an old saying to connect to it—some sort of warning or word of wisdom. Most of the time I paid little attention to Gran's old sayings. They were just a part of her—actually, they were a part of her charm. But it was uncanny how often her warnings came true.

After graduating from high school, I got a job in the office at Bendix Industries. By working during the day and attending evening classes at our community college, I was able to continue my education. That resulted in my being given promotions at Bendix.

When I told Gran my plans to get an apartment of my own she encouraged me to do it. I'd been concerned that she would insist that I stay with her. But she understood my desire to be independent. She surprised me with an announcement of her own: she had been offered a chance to sell her house—the only reason she would turn down the offer was so she could continue to provide a home for me. So in the end it worked out fine. I got my own apartment, and Gran moved into a senior citizen's apartment building.

She quickly made friends with other senior ladies in her building and, she remained active—going on short bus tours with them, playing bingo in the activity room. She no longer could drive, but each Sunday morning she climbed onto the van that stopped by to pick her up and take her to the church she'd attended for a lifetime. I was so proud of her for all she was doing at this advanced age.

Although Gran and I no longer lived together, we remained in close contact. I went to see her at least once a week. I took her shopping, to movies, or out to dinner.

Each time I started to date a new man, I took him to visit Gran. If she didn't approve of him, I knew there was some flaw in him. In time her opinion always proved to be true. When I brought Marv to her apartment, she was very sweet to him. She gave him some of her home-baked cookies and chatted amiably with him. Later she told me, "That young man isn't sincere. He has a wondering soul."

"A wandering soul?" I asked her with a laugh. "Gran, what is that?"

"His eyes—his posture... He squints his eyes . . . that means he isn't sincere. He doesn't stand straight—that means he will not live straight. You cannot trust him, Valerie."

I laughed at yet another of her old sayings. But a week later, I knew Gran's prediction was accurate when I saw Marv having lunch with one of the girls who worked with him.

I'll never forget the day Sterling Billingsley walked into my office. I was almost buried under the stack of work that my boss, Mr. Richards, had piled on me. It seemed that the harder I worked the less I got accomplished. I felt like one of Gran's old sayings: "The faster I go, the behinder I get."

I knew I was a capable, efficient worker but today was turning out to be a nightmare. Some of the data Mr. Richards had given me was obsolete and after I entered it into my computer and realized the inaccuracy, I tried to delete it. I have no idea what I did wrong. But one moment my computer was working fine—and the next moment it was showing weird things on the monitor screen.

I ended up having to call for a computer technician to unscramble the mess I'd created. That was how I met Sterling Billingsley. He walked into the office, looked at my computer, did some of this, some of that, and a few other things—and poof! My computer was working good as new.

When he saw the look of relief on my face he stood and laughed at me. "You really were worried, weren't you?" he grinned.

"Yes, I was," I admitted. "I have to get this work done today and with an uncooperative computer I was getting nowhere fast."

"Well, computers can be temperamental," he smiled. "I think they act that way sometimes just to get extra attention."

I laughed. "I think you're right about that."

"Hey, you can smile," he said as he stood looking at me.

"Well, I finally have something to smile about." I grinned. "My computer is working all right again."

"Want to celebrate?"

I glanced at the tall man standing beside my desk. "Celebrate? What do you mean?"

"We should celebrate that your computer is behaving again. We should go get some lunch."

I smiled up at him. "Sounds like a good idea, but I cannot leave this station until I get at least halfway through this pile of junk on my desk."

He leaned down so that he was on eye-level with me. I saw that his dark eyes had tiny glints of gold in them. I smelled the scent of his aftershave lotion. I saw his strong broad shoulders.

"If you can't have lunch with me then how about having dinner with me? We can take our time and celebrate then. You won't have to hurry back to work. See, that's an even better plan."

He stood up, picked up his workcase and told me, "I'll pick you up right here—at the front door to Bendix Industries—when you get off work."

Before I could answer, he had left.

That evening Sterling Billingsley and I went to the Silver Waterfall and had a wonderful meal. Our table was near a large window that overlooked a lovely garden. I enjoyed the food, the atmosphere—and most especially, the company of a truly interesting, handsome man.

From the very first, Sterling and I seemed to have a special bond. We had a similar sense of humor, we both liked taking long drives in the country, and we enjoyed watching auto racing on TV. Both of us enjoyed reading and often discussed some novel or autobiography we'd read. We attended church together at the same church Gran attended. We offered to pick her up and take her with us on Sunday mornings, but she preferred to ride the church van. I think it gave her a feeling of independence. So we let her do as she wished but sometimes we sat with her during the service.

I think I knew from that first evening we spent at the Silver Waterfall that Sterling was the man I had been waiting for so long. We seemed to be made for each other. I felt so complete and whole when I was with him. When we were apart, I felt as though something was missing.

Christmas Eve Sterling asked me to marry him. I didn't hesitate for a second when I agreed to be his wife. We sat in the glow of my small

4

Christmas tree and began making plans for our wedding and for our future life together. We would both continue to work. Sterling would move into my apartment and we would begin to save money toward the house we eventually would buy.

"Let's get married tomorrow!" Sterling said eagerly. "You can be my favorite Christmas gift!"

I laughed at his challenge. "That is too soon!" I declared. I knew he was teasing but I understood his eagerness to get married as soon as possible.

When he suggested we have a Valentine's Day wedding, I was enchanted with the idea. I'd always considered Valentine's Day to be one of the most romantic times—it would be perfect for our wedding day. We would have a small wedding at our church—just a few close friends and of course, Gran had to be there. It wouldn't be complete without her.

I could hardly wait to share our good news with her. I certainly never expected the kind of response I got from her when I told her about our wedding plans.

"Valerie, you cannot get married on Valentine's Day!" she'd insisted. When she warned me about the Valentine's Day Curse, I shrugged off her words. I loved her dearly and I really respected her vast knowledge of old sayings. I knew they were words of wisdom. I knew that too often her warnings came true. For a brief moment, her words made me pause. Then I whisked them away. That "curse" might apply to someone else—but not to Sterling and me. The love Sterling and I had for each other would keep our marriage strong forever.

Our wedding day was indeed special. We had a small reception in a private party room at the Silver Waterfall because that was the first place we had ever gone together.

With each passing day, I knew I loved Sterling more. When I awoke in the morning and saw him laying beside me my heart sang with joy. When we both got home from work late in the afternoon, he helped me with getting a meal on the table and we shared good food and good conversation at the end of a busy day. We ended the day in each other's arms, secure in the special love we shared.

Before I realized it, we were celebrating our first anniversary. Of course, we went to the Silver Waterfall for the event. He looked so handsome sitting across from me in his dark blue suit. I'd had my hair done in a special way earlier that day and with my new dress, I knew he had to be pleased with me. Later when we got home, I knew he was pleased with me.

Spring moved in bringing new soft green leaves, and the heat of summer began to pour down on our small town. Sterling began working extra hours at his job. He was sent to Chicago a couple of times to attend seminars to update his computing skills. It seemed he was gone from home more and more. The apartment was so empty when he was gone. The nights were so long and lonely.

As autumn began to turn the leaves to gold, a new school year began. Sterling was asked to volunteer a few hours a week at the high school to help computer students with their classes. I was proud of him for contributing his extensive knowledge to help teenagers.

Because he was gone even more these days I decided to spend some of my extra after-work time doing volunteer work at the local library tutoring children in reading skills. I really enjoyed working with the little ones. They came to me apprehensive about the way letters formed words and words conveyed interesting ideas. As they gained understanding they gained confidence and soon they found reading to be a wonderful adventure.

The weather turned cold and snow covered our town. Sterling seemed to be gone even more these days. His boss sent him out of town for more computer training. He headed up a committee at church. It seemed it was always something—his job or volunteer work or church work—that was cutting into our time together.

I was just as busy as he was. Sometimes I worked overtime at the office. I was still helping the children at the library and I, too, was on not one, but two, committees at church. I began to wish that the good Lord had created eight days instead of seven so that I would have at least one day a week to relax.

In spite of our busy schedules, I made it a point to keep in touch with Gran. Now, however, it was usually just me who went to visit her or take her to the mall. She seldom saw Sterling because he was seldom home.

We had Gran come to our house for Christmas Day. We had a delightful time together opening gifts, sharing a wonderful meal and watching a Christmas movie on TV.

Late in the afternoon, I drove her back to her apartment. Just before she got out of my car she turned to me and asked, "Valerie, is everything all right?"

"All right?" I asked. I had no idea what she was talking about. "Of course, everything is alright."

"Really?" she questioned. "Are you and Sterling getting along okay?"

"Gran, you know we are. We are so happy together. Sterling is the best thing that ever happened to me . . . besides you, of course."

She shook her head. "I'm concerned, Valerie. Something is wrong. I can tell."

"Gran, what are you talking about? You were with us all day today. Didn't you have a good time? I know that Sterling and I were so glad to have you with us. You made our Christmas special—just by being with us."

"That's not what I'm talking about, Valerie," she said. "There seems to be a distance between you and Sterling. I might be an old lady—but I can sense these things. I want you to be happy, Honey. Both of you. But I can feel that something is not as it should be."

"Gran, we are fine. You worry too much."

"You don't have enough sunshine in your life, Valerie."

"Sunshine?" Now what was she talking about?

She explained, "The old saying is 'A day without love is like a day without sunshine.' I think some of the sunshine has gone away from you and Sterling."

"Gran! How can you say that? I'm telling you. Sterling and I are fine. And yes, we do have 'sunshine' in our lives."

After she went into her apartment building, I started to drive home. Her words kept going through my mind. I couldn't understand her reasoning. Maybe she was getting old and senile. All this talk about no sunshine—no love. I knew I loved Sterling and I knew he loved me. I pushed away my grandmother's nonsensical words.

After the hectic pace of the holidays, life settled back into its old pattern. Both Sterling and I were going night and day—to one place or another. It seemed there were just not enough hours in the day. Often we both just dropped into bed, too exhausted even to say "Good night." I missed the feel of his arms around me, the magical closeness of him. But it is difficult to hug or cuddle with someone who is already asleep beside you. So I turned over and hugged my pillow and sometimes I shed a few tears.

Tomorrow will be better, I promised myself as I drifted off into a troubled sleep.

But tomorrow was not better. Tomorrow was just a repeat of yesterday—and the day before. I couldn't recall the last time Sterling and I had spent a quiet evening sitting together on the couch watching TV or went to a movie or went out to dinner. There wasn't time for such luxuries—not when there was another committee meeting to get to or a lesson to prepare for the children at the library.

Our second anniversary came and went—but we never got to celebrate it together because Sterling's boss had sent him out of town again.

One Saturday morning in early March, I stood at the living room window looking out at the cold, gray dismal rain that fell from the sky. The weather matched my mood perfectly. This winter season seemed to be lasting forever. I really wished I could see a day with some sunshine.

Sunshine. Just the mention of that word brought Gran's words whispering back into my mind. "A day without love is like a day without sunshine." I could still hear her soft voice saying, "I think some of the sunshine has gone away from you and Sterling."

I turned from the window and stood with my arms wrapped tightly about me in an effort to defend myself from the emotions that sifted down over me.

I walked to the sofa and sat down. I used to enjoy Saturday morning. Sterling and I used to get in the car and take long, early morning drives and watch the world wake up. We'd stop at some little diner and have breakfast and we talked and laughed and marveled at the wonder of being together.

On Saturday afternoons, we used to go to the market and do our grocery shopping together. That was fun, too. Sterling would pick up a can of something that he knew I would never ever eat and he'd threaten to put it into the shopping cart. I would counter his threat by taking out of the cart something I knew he really wanted—such as the delicious chocolate cake from the store bakery. Then we would compromise—he put the dumb item back on the shelf and I returned the cake box to the cart. And we laughed. Yes, we used to laugh.

As I sat on the sofa, I realized that we didn't laugh anymore. We didn't go grocery shopping anymore. We each just picked up a few things on our way home from work--anything—just so we'd have something to put on the table for dinner

Dinner. That was a joke. We didn't have dinner together these days. He often had to work late or had to go over to the church for a committee meeting. Often, after he was done at work, he went to the high school where they had adult evening classes. He helped adults in their efforts to become acquainted with computers. Of course, I was proud of him for reaching out and helping others. His kind, generous heart was one of the things I loved about him.

Now I sat alone on the sofa and I cried—I wasn't sure what I was crying about—I just knew that I was so lonely. I felt so empty--as though a part of me had vanished somehow. What was wrong? Why did I feel like this? I felt as though something had gone out of my life . . . just sort of faded away.

Fade away. Where had I heard that phrase before? I knew I'd heard it sometime—someplace. When I couldn't recall, I dismissed it from my mind. Well, I tried to dismiss it—but the rest of the day it kept whispering through my thoughts.

I was putting clothes into the washer, and the words "fade away" moved through my mind. As I was running the sweeper and dusting, I seemed to hear those words.

Sterling called me in the afternoon to tell me he would be late getting home—again. He was still at the church, still involved in a committee meeting. When he was done with that, he was going back to his office for awhile.

I hung up the phone and dropped onto the sofa. I was weary of all this going, going, going. It never seemed to end. Just when I thought things would get better, they seemed to get worse. One of Gran's old sayings came to my mind: "The more things change the more they stay the same." How true that was.

I smiled as I thought about all the hundreds of times Gran had told me her old sayings—and how often they had come true. I was really blessed to have been raised by Gran. Because of her, I'd had a wonderful childhood. And because of her, I bet I knew more old sayings than anyone else.

Then I stopped laughing. I sat up straight on the couch. That was where I heard that phrase! The day I told Gran that Sterling and I were going to be married on Valentine's Day! She'd been so upset. She almost demanded that we change the date. And she'd recited one of her predictions: "If you marry on Valentine's Day your love is sure to fade away."

She had called it the Valentine's Day Curse. And she'd become quite agitated when I told her we didn't believe in that stuff and we were not changing our wedding plans. I'd forgotten all about all of that—until just now. Then it all came rushing back into my mind.

I leaned back against the soft cushion of the sofa and closed my eyes. I could see Gran looking straight at me and warning me. Then I recalled her concern for Sterling and me last Christmas when I drove her home. She'd told me that "some of the sunshine had gone away from Sterling and me."

I'd always brushed aside those warnings and predictions. Some of them did have a grain of wisdom in them—but many of them were just "old wives' tales."

Now I wondered. Was there such a thing as a "Valentine's Day Curse"? No, of course, there wasn't. I knew better than to think that way.

But as I considered the overall picture, I could see that some of the sunshine had gone out of our marriage. Something had indeed faded away from the relationship we had enjoyed so much when we first became man and wife. Sometimes, I hardly even felt like a wife these days.

I started to cry . . . just sat there on the sofa and wept—for something that Sterling and I had once had but which now seemed to be gone. I felt a sense of loss . . . emptiness. And I didn't know what to do about it.

I was still sitting there when Sterling came home. He took his coat off, hung it in the hall closet and dropped onto the sofa beside me.

"You okay?" he asked. "Have you been crying?"

I didn't answer. I didn't know how to tell him I was wondering about that dumb old curse. Was it coming true? I knew I was being irrational—but I felt irrational. Nothing was making sense to me. I had no idea how we'd reached this point in our lives and I had no idea how to get beyond this point.

"Valerie, what's wrong?" Sterling asked. "Are you ill? Is Gran ill? Did you get word from her that something is wrong with her?"

I shook my head. "No—nothing like that. I'm not sick. Gran is fine. I talked to her yesterday and she is okay."

"That's good," he sounded relieved. "But why have you been crying?"

I sat up and turned to look at him. I took a good long look at him—something I hadn't done for a while. He looked tired, weary. "Are you okay?" I asked.

"Sure, I'm fine."

"No, I don't think you are fine," I told him. "And I don't think I am fine. And I don't think we are fine."

He looked at me, confusion touching his dark eyes. "What are you talking about?"

"You will laugh at me," I told him. "If I tell you—you will think I am foolish, and silly—and you'll laugh at me."

"Try me," he challenged. "And I promise not to laugh," he added.

Before I realized it, I was telling him about how lonely I was, how much I missed him all the time. I told him about Gran's words about the "sunshine going away" from us. Once I started talking to him, I couldn't stop. I reminded him about Gran's not wanting us to marry on Valentine's Day because of that so-called curse—but we had married then anyway. Now I wondered if maybe—just maybe—there was something to it. Because our marriage and our love seemed to have faded away.

Then I was crying again. And to my amazement, Sterling had tears in his eyes. He pulled me close to him, wrapped his long strong arms around me and held me so tightly—something that he hadn't done for quite awhile. There had never been time to sit together and hold onto each other and snuggle and feel each other's heart beat.

Then it was his turn to talk. He told me how alone he'd felt lately—in spite of his being involved in so many things with so many people. That activity, those people could not fill a void in his heart. Only I could do that. But lately both of us had been so busy that we hadn't had time to connect with each other at any time on any level.

We sat and talked a long time—there on the couch—with the March rain falling outside our living room window. It felt so good just to be together—to be open and honest with each other.

10

After we had both talked, we sat together quietly. Sterling put his arms around me, and I rested my head on his strong shoulder. For the first time in a long time, I felt connected to him. I felt that some great heavy weight had been lifted from my heart and mind.

After sitting there awhile I moved out of the shelter of Sterling's arm and turned to look at him. The look of weariness and stress I had seen when he first came home was gone. I could see a difference in him—and I knew I could feel a difference in me.

"So—what do we do about all this?" I asked. "We have finally realized that we have a problem—we have defined the problem—so what do we do to correct the problem?"

"I think we call the problem 'being too busy'." he said as he reached over to brush a strand of hair from my forehead. "So to 'solve' the problem we have to be less busy. We have to spend more time with each other."

I sighed. How did we do that? I worked every day. He worked every day. I still helped tutor children at the library. He still served as a computer instructor at the high school. We both served on several church committees. How did we get out from under all the assignments we had?

We spent a lot of time discussing our options. We decided to eliminate some things from our "Must Do" list.

We both agreed to refuse any more overtime at our jobs. We both decided we would volunteer only a few evenings a month instead of once or twice each week. We both decided to resign from a few church committees. Being on one committee was acceptable. Being on more than that was cutting into our time together too much—so that was not acceptable.

After talking so much, making such major decisions, re-arranging our priorities we both had one problem left to deal with. We were hungry!

"Go get yourself prettied up," Sterling said as he helped me up from the sofa. "We are going out to celebrate!"

"Celebrate?" I asked as I stood beside him. "What are we celebrating?"

"Well, once upon a time, several years ago I asked you out to dinner to celebrate my getting your computer to work properly. This time I am asking you out to dinner to celebrate the fact that we are getting our make our marriage work properly." His voice had a light tone—something I had not heard for much too long.

Of course, we went to the Silver Waterfall—and we sat at the table near the window that looked out over the now barren garden. But I didn't notice that—I couldn't take my eyes off the handsome man in the dark blue suit who sat opposite me.

11

We enjoyed a scrumptious meal, listened to softly muted music, and held hands across the table like newlyweds. I think that our marriage had a new beginning that evening. This is where it had all begun—sitting here on our first date several years ago. We were rediscovering each other, realizing that a love that might have almost "faded away" was fresh and new—and like the flowers in the garden beyond the window, our love would continue to grow and bloom

The next year when Valentine's Day arrived, Sterling and I renewed our wedding vows. Gran was with us and she beamed as she watched us promise again to love and cherish each other as long as we both would live.

Of course, Gran had some "words of wisdom" to cover this wonderful occasion. As she gave us each a loving hug she said, "A wedding vow that you renew will bring a lifetime of love to you."

"Gran!" I smiled as I returned her hug. "You never told me that old saying before. It is really a special one."

"Well," she laughed in her own special way, "I never had a chance to tell it to anyone before. This is the first time I attended a wedding renewal. And as for it being special—well, to me the most special thing is the fact that you and Sterling are happy. Like the old saying says: 'Your happiness is my happiness'."

I was glad Gran got to live long enough to see Sterling and me build a strong marriage. She also got to see our two children—Paul and Ruth.

Although Gran is gone from us now, she still lives on in our hearts—and in her old sayings that still echo in my mind everyone in awhile. As she said, "Hearts and homes that are entwined in love receive blessings from the Lord above."

The End

VALENTINE'S DAY
LOVE GAME
My Meddling Mom

"**M**om, you're just plain biased," I said, with loving exasperation as I cut up another tomato, and dropped it in the salad bowl.

"Of course I am, honey," my mother said, as she straightened and looked over the refrigerator door at me. "But no matter what you say, I still think you're beautiful, Victoria, so I don't know why you wouldn't expect to get a Valentine's Day card from some nice young man this year. Or even some flowers."

"Because I don't have a boyfriend," I quipped, feeling more like a teenager than twenty-five years old. My mother still believed a woman needed a man to be complete. Any man by the sounds of it, I thought, ruefully. "And I'm not beautiful."

"Who's not beautiful?" Josh Kingsley said, sliding open the patio door and stepping inside as if he owned the place. A strand of blond hair flopped down over his brow, making him look carelessly handsome in a nerdy sort of way.

I smiled sweetly and said, "None of your business."

But as always, his constant presence in my parents' house irritated me. He'd been my older brother's best friend since forever, but did they have to invite him over whenever I came home from the city for the weekend? Didn't he have a life of his own? Sure, as partners in a small computer company, Josh and Matt liked to get together to talk over things—but didn't they get enough of that at work?

Josh pushed up the wire rims that had slipped down the bridge of his nose.

"You're talking about Vicki, aren't you?"

I gritted my teeth.

"It's Victoria, if you don't mind."

And that was another thing. He still called me Vicki when I had specifically asked to be called Victoria. Vicki sounded like a schoolgirl, not a woman who'd worked hard to get to the position of office manager. That was the trouble with Josh. He'd never taken me seriously. I'd always been Matt's kid sister to him.

My mother gave a nervous laugh and shoved some lettuce into my hands.

"Josh, I was just saying I couldn't believe no one would give Vicki—"

She shot me a look.

13

"Er . . . I mean, Victoria, a Valentine's Day card this year. I mean, she's never received a card from any man."

Gee, thanks for telling the world, Mom! I thought. It sounded like I'd never had a boyfriend, either.

"I don't want a Valentine's Day card, Mom. I couldn't care less if I never get one."

My mother was having none of that. Not when she had an audience in Josh, now.

"But every girl should get at least one Valentine's Day card in her life," she said, as if it were more important than breathing.

I began pulling the lettuce leaves apart with more force than necessary.

"Why?"

"Because every woman deserves to be appreciated," Josh said quietly, making my eyes widen in astonishment. He sounded like he knew what he was talking about.

Yeah, right. Since when had Josh started noticing women?

I grimaced. Okay, so he'd probably started noticing women long ago. But when had they started noticing him?

Just then he came around the kitchen table toward me, and for the first time, I became aware of his clothes. Good grief! Would the real Josh Kingsley please stand up? Denim jeans instead of trousers? And not only was he wearing them, he was wearing them very well indeed. They hugged him like a second skin.

Feeling weak-kneed, I hurriedly threw the lettuce in the salad bowl and began to toss it. I felt hot all over.

Well, it was summer in Australia.

"See. There you are then," my mother declared, forcing me back to the conversation. "You're a woman, darling; so you deserve to be appreciated. Josh says so."

Good for Josh.

Not!

"I'm already appreciated, Mom."

"By whom?"

Josh's tone seemed to demand rather than question. In my surprise, I tossed the salad too high—causing some of it to land on the tiled floor. If I didn't know better, I'd think he was jealous.

But that couldn't be true. To be jealous, a person had to care. And Josh had never cared about me. Not in that way.

Quickly, I bent to pick the food off the floor, and threw it in the garbage.

"Well, my boss appreciates me . . . and my friends. My family, too." I looked pointedly at my mother and gave a wry smile. "Most of the time, anyway."

14

Josh moved closer to me in the kitchen area, his presence seeming to fill the small space. "Yeah, but there's just something about being appreciated by that special person in your life, don't you think?"

A funny feeling washed over me. It must've been from Josh's aftershave. I liked its spicy scent.

"You're talking from experience, no doubt?"

He stopped dead, his jaw taut.

"I don't spend my whole time in front of a computer, you know."

"Really?"

Hmm. I didn't remember him wearing aftershave, before. Of course, I'd never noticed a lot of things about him before today.

What was wrong with me, for goodness sake? It reminded me of that odd feeling I'd had, lately. A sort of strange restlessness, as if something were missing from my life.

Yet how could that be? I was happy. Just because I didn't have a boyfriend. . . . Now, look what my mother had started!

"So, who's the lucky woman?" I said as casually as I could.

His face closed up even more than usual.

"No one you'd know."

"It's serious, is it?" I couldn't stop myself from asking.

His lips twisted.

"You make it sound like a disease."

"As long as it's not contagious."

But I was shocked to realize that suddenly, I wouldn't mind being caught by this man. And that was a totally unacceptable idea. Josh was almost like a brother to me.

"Don't worry, Victoria. I'm sure you're immune."

He turned stiffly, and strode back to the patio door, then disappeared outside to the others without a second glance—leaving me standing there with my mouth open.

I turned to look at my mother, her eyes wide with surprise.

"What's the matter with him?"

My mother harrumphed.

"I may be wrong, but I think he's in love."

"And?"

I ignored a strange sinking feeling in my stomach. Josh in love? How can that be?

"The feeling's not reciprocated."

"Oh."

Why did I suddenly feel better? Because the woman obviously wasn't right for him, that's why. Josh had always been a complex person. Only a woman who loved him would understand that.

Not that I loved him, I quickly added. I just understood him, that was all.

"Well, I'd have to be blind not to notice what a hunk he's grown into," I said, trying to keep the conversation light, then I froze when I caught something like satisfaction cross my mother's face.

Giving an inward groan, I pretended to have an intense interest in pouring the dressing onto the salad, but I could feel my cheeks growing warm.

There was a long silence; then, my mother picked up the tray of meat for the cookout and headed for the patio door.

"Sometimes, a woman doesn't want to see what's right in front of her," she said with quiet emphasis.

Startled, I looked up just as she stepped outside, her back ramrod straight—like Josh's had been.

All at once my pulse began to pound. Was my mother talking about me? That I didn't see what was in front of my eyes?

Ridiculous. My mother must be getting desperate for those grandbabies if she thinks Josh is in love with me. Instinctively, I knew if Josh loved me, then nothing would stop him from coming after me. Hadn't I seen his dogged determination, time and time again, over the years when he'd been working on the computer and unable to solve a problem?

I mentally shook my head. No, there was no way that Josh loved me. Josh had never come after me, not even when I'd moved to the city five years ago.

And he'd never even tried to kiss me. Not once. Didn't that say something? Yet, my heart hammered foolishly at the thought of it.

Pushing aside the unsettling thought of Josh kissing me, I grabbed the salad bowl, raised my chin high, and headed for the patio. I just hoped my mother didn't get any more silly ideas.

Josh and me?

Never in a million years.

For all my determination, I found myself peeking looks at him during dinner. Why had I never noticed what a nice smile he had before? Or that the color of his eyes were blue? Or that he was the first to offer my mother one of the comfortable chairs, so she could watch the sun set on the horizon? Or, how well he held his own during a debate with my father about taxes?

And that was all my mother's fault, I decided, sipping the wine, but not really tasting it. If my mother hadn't put this crazy idea in my head about Josh being in love with me, then I'd merely be enjoying a summer evening with my family.

Now that feeling of restlessness had returned. But I still couldn't put my finger on it. It was just a feeling deep inside me.

Of course, that probably had something to do with the daggers my mother and Josh kept sending me, I thought in wry amusement. The way they were looking at me would make anyone think I'd started smoking, again.

"Hey, why not take Vicki out to dinner on Friday?" I heard my brother say, which almost made me choke on my drink.

I coughed.

"Wh ... what?"

Matt shook his head at Josh.

"She hasn't been listening to a word we've been saying." He turned to me. "Josh is going into the city on Friday for a job interview. I was telling him he should stay and take you out to dinner."

I blinked, then focused my gaze on Josh.

"An interview?"

I wasn't even going to address the dinner part just yet.

Josh's blue eyes pierced the distance between us.

"I've decided to move to the city and take a job with a big computer company."

"But . . . but why?"

My brain wasn't working. This was too much to take in.

"It's time to make a change." He saw me glance at my brother. "Don't worry, Matt doesn't mind. We've got a couple of others working for us who can take over for me." He shrugged his broad shoulders. "Who knows? I may not even pass the interview."

"Of course, you will," my mother said, obviously shocked he'd even suggest such a thing. "Now tell Victoria what time you'll pick her up for dinner?"

"Mom!"

"Honey, ssh."

My mouth tightened.

"Has it occurred to anyone that I might already have a date on Friday night? It is Valentine's Day, you know."

Not that I considered this would be a date with Josh. It was an engagement, that's all.

No, on second thought, that sounded too personal.

Call it an appointment.

"Do you?"

This time, it was Josh who spoke.

"Um . . . no . . . but that's not the point."

I shot a dark look at the others, although my heart softened when I looked at my father. He was a dear. If ever I were to marry, it would be to a man like him.

Not that I was thinking about marriage. I didn't even have a boyfriend.

"My family is under the impression that I don't have a social life. Let me tell you I have a very full life. I go to art classes once a week and aerobics twice—"

17

"Honey, we know all that," my mother cut across me. "But doesn't it make sense that with Josh in the city on Friday night and knowing no one, you'd want him to spend time with family?" She sent Josh a motherly smile. "He is part of the family, after all."

"Part of the furniture, you mean?" Josh teased back, and I felt something shift in the region of my heart.

Heck, I wasn't sure I could put up with living in the same city as this man again—let alone sit across from him in an intimate restaurant!

Maybe I'd suggest a fast-food joint.

"Well, what do you think, Vicki?" Josh said, suddenly smiling at me with what I thought was a challenge in his eyes. "Are you up for dinner on Friday?"

All at once, I had the feeling he was asking for more than he was saying. I gulped. A relationship? Could my mother have been right after all?

As if someone else had taken over my body, I looked at his gorgeous blue eyes and terrific smile, and found myself nodding in agreement.

I guess it wouldn't hurt to find out.

Throughout the following week, I told myself I was merely going to dinner with my brother's best friend, but when I entered the hotel and saw Josh waiting for me near the restaurant door, I felt giddy all of a sudden.

He looked up then, his eyes flaring as if a light had been switched on inside him. My heart skipped a beat as I moved across the foyer toward him, feeling breathless and ridiculously shy.

He lowered his head and kissed my cheek.

"I wasn't sure you'd come."

My skin tingled where his lips had touched.

"I didn't want to disappoint Mom," I joked, weakly.

His eyes held mine.

"Your mom wouldn't have been the only disappointed one."

Oh my. What could I say to that?

"Um . . . did you get the job?"

"Yes. I'll tell you all about it over dinner."

And he did. I could see he was excited about moving to the city, but there was something more in his eyes. Something that made my pulse go crazy. I tried to ignore it throughout the evening, but that was like trying to ignore Christmas.

We'd just finished our meal when a woman stopped by our table selling flowers. After giving me a long look, Josh bought the last long-stemmed red rose, making my stomach dance with butterflies.

Once we were alone, he placed the gorgeous rose in front of me.

"For you, Vicki," he murmured.

I licked my lips, my heart pounding in my ears.

"Why?" I said, somewhat stupidly.

"Why?" His eyes filled with a touch of amusement. "Because every woman deserves flowers—of course."

"Oh." I quickly hid my disappointment. He was doing this for dear Mom's sake, not mine. "I can finally tell Mom a man gave me flowers on Valentine's Day," I joked, as I tried to act normal while inhaling its heady perfume. "Well, one flower, anyway. I wonder if that makes up for not getting a Valentine's Day card again this year?" I quipped.

Only he didn't smile.

"Hey, you don't think—"

He paused.

"Vicki, you crazy woman; this has nothing to do with your mother."

I gasped. Did that mean.... Could he be saying....

"Vicki, this flower is from me. I was going to get you a card, but I decided I'd rather tell you how I feel in my own words—not someone else's. This flower is just for starters."

"Wh . . . what?"

"Vicki, this flower is from me. The man who loves you. The man who's always loved you."

I swallowed hard, hardly daring to breath.

"You're kidding, right?"

"Do I look like I'm kidding?"

I stared into his eyes. No, he didn't. Far from it.

"Oh Josh."

At that moment I knew I loved him, too. And not like a brother either. He was so handsome, so masculine, yet a kind man. I knew it wasn't just his looks that attracted me. He was a genuinely nice person—inside and out. Just like my dad. Josh got to his feet, took out his wallet, and threw some money on the table.

"Come on. Let's find someplace quiet. I want to kiss you."

I had no objection to that. None at all.

A few minutes later, he opened a door near the elevator marked "Ballroom."

"Good. It's empty," he said, pushing me gently through the doorway before closing the door behind us, shutting out the world.

And then, I watched his head lower toward me, wanting to say so many things, but needing to kiss him first.

I raised my mouth up to him. Words could wait. The kiss couldn't.

Long moments later, we finally came up for air.

Feeling something thorny sticking in my chest, I looked down at the flower still in my hand.

"Oh no, my rose is getting squashed."

His smile held pure love.

19

"Then I'll buy you more, sweetheart. I intend to say it with flowers as often as I can from now on."

I was still pinching myself.

"Say what with flowers?" I teased, huskily.

"That I love you, Victoria Milner. More than I can say."

I reached up and lovingly brushed aside that stray lock of hair off his forehead.

"Joshua Kingsley, I love you back."

He chuckled and kissed me again, and I melted into him, as my world fell into place. I had the feeling I wasn't going to feel restless, anymore. And that wasn't because I needed a man by my side like my mother believed. But because I needed one man: Josh.

I had finally come full circle to the place I belonged: in Josh's arms, and in his heart.

My mother would be pleased. . . .

The End

OUR SCHOOL DANCE
Led Me To His Heart

"Gloria, you did such a great job last year that I'd like you to coordinate this year's Sweetheart Dance." Peter's words were like rubbing salt into a wound. The last thing I wanted to do was work on the high school's Valentine's dance. Yet there was no way I could refuse the principal's request.

"I'd be happy to help this year." I forced a smile on my lips and hoped my voice rang with more enthusiasm than I felt. Just when I thought things were bad enough, Peter told me who'd be working with me.

"I've asked Mitch Anderson to help you. Since he hasn't been here long, he hasn't worked on many projects. This is a good opportunity for him." Mitch was the science teacher that my friend, Sally, and I had nicknamed Mr. Grumps. We called him that because he never smiled. At the beginning of the school year we couldn't remember his name.

Peter and I talked about some of the dance details and other school business before he headed toward the door of my office. "Have fun with the dance," he said. "I know you did last year."

That was last year—a whole lifetime ago when I still believed in love and happy relationships.

I gazed at the bookcase across the room. The photo album from last year's dance rested on the lowest shelf. I'd never looked in the album, but I knew what was in it. Besides the usual pictures of the students in their party finery, there were pictures of Bruce and me. We were married then, and he'd come to the dance to help chaperone.

It had been a romantic evening with fancy dresses, glittery decorations, and soft music. I wore a new red dress and matching shoes that had been well worth the price from all the compliments I'd received. Bruce and I even had time for a couple of dances. In his arms, dancing under the balloons and hearts above us, I felt like the most loved woman in the world.

To me, our Valentine's celebration was only beginning at the Sweetheart Dance. I'd planned for us to have our own Valentine's celebration when we got home. I had a bottle of white wine chilling in the refrigerator and I'd bought a new lacy nightgown that I knew would make Bruce's heart race.

The telephone was ringing when we walked into the house. It was midnight and I immediately feared that something had happened to Bruce's parents or mine. I was still wearing my coat when I picked up the phone. I didn't recognize the woman's voice and she was hard to understand. She was crying and sounded drunk, so I thought she must've misdialed until I finally understood that she wanted to talk to Bruce.

I can still remember watching him on the telephone as he talked to her. Chills ran down my spine and my stomach twisted as I stood in the kitchen wearing my coat, listening to him tell her that he was sorry he couldn't be with her that night. Every once in a while he'd look helplessly at me. I'd thought my marriage was so wonderful, so perfect. How could I have been so blind?

Instead of the romantic celebration I'd planned, I spent hours listening to Bruce try to explain how he was in love with two women. He'd been staying with me because he couldn't make up his mind about what to do. After many explanations and much discussion, I told Bruce to pack his things. I threw the Valentine from him with its loving words into the garbage. I gave my red dress to Goodwill and I returned the nightgown to the department store, since I'd never worn it and I never would.

I'd planned on ignoring Valentine's Day this year. Everyone I'd dated since my breakup with Bruce had been a disappointment. I had no romantic plans for the evening and the holiday held bad memories for me. Instead, I was in the thick of planning a Valentine's dance. With Mr. Grumps.

Maybe Mitch would turn out to be friendlier than he appeared. Sally and I didn't really know him. She taught English and seldom went to the science building. I was the school librarian, but Mitch never came to the library. He didn't have reading lists for his students, nor did he have the need for me to order books. I turned to my computer and sent Mitch an e-mail asking to meet with him.

A couple of hours later I walked into Mitch's classroom. The room was lined with lab tables and stools. Chemical odors hovering around the room reminded me of my days in chemistry lab. Mitch looked up from his desk and stood up to greet me. As I sat down in the chair next to his desk, I couldn't help thinking that he was a nice-looking man. It was too bad he wasn't friendlier.

A picture of him and a woman was prominently displayed on his desk. I had to look twice to be sure he was the man in the picture. That man was smiling and there was a light in his eyes that was clearly missing from the man sitting behind the desk talking to me.

"I'm new at arranging dances," Mitch said, putting his elbows on the desk, "but I'm willing to learn and do whatever is necessary." He sounded sincere, but again he didn't appear friendly.

I explained about the dance being an annual event and some the details about our roles. As I talked, he had a few questions but not

22

many. When I was done with my explanations I set last year's photo album on his desk. "You may want to look at last year's pictures to see what we did. This year's dance falls right on Valentine's Day, so we'll probably have a big turnout this year."

He nodded and flipped open the album.

"You can keep the album until we meet with the student committee later this week." I stood up and prepared to leave. "You're welcome to bring a date or your wife to the dance."

He looked up from the book and his gaze met mine. "I'll be coming alone."

I didn't know what to say, so I nodded and told him I'd see him later in the week.

That was fun, I told myself as I walked back to the library. Mitch wasn't rude—he just wasn't much of a conversationalist. Talking to him was like talking to a dead man. If he hadn't asked a few questions and nodded his head occasionally, I wouldn't have known he was listening at all. I hoped he was sincere in his offer to help.

A couple of days later, Mitch and I met with the student committee. I'd been dreading the meeting because I knew how energetic and lively teenage girls could be about a dance, especially a Sweetheart Dance on Valentine's Day. Mitch had just sat down at the table when Tammy, the school president, and her friends swept into the conference room. As I'd expected, their faces were filled with high energy and excitement.

"I saw this darling dress at the mall," Tammy was saying.

"I've got to go on an emergency diet before I even look for a dress," another girl said.

"Hi, everyone," I said, interrupting the chatter.

"Mrs. Austin, I'm so glad you're coordinating our dance," Tammy said as she pulled out a chair. "We had a lot of fun last year. Didn't we?"

"Yes, we did," I agreed, and moved the conversation away from last year. "Since this is your second year on the committee, you'll have a lot of good ideas."

My words opened Pandora's box. Within seconds the conference room table was covered with pictures from magazines, red foil hearts, garlands with tiny cupids, balloons, and more. I looked at Mitch across the table. His eyes were round but serious. I remembered the picture of him on the desk with the lively eyes and bright smile. I wished that man was seated here today instead of Mr. Grumps. I shouldn't be thinking about him anyway, so I forced my attention to the myriad of decorations on the table. Just looking at them made my heart ache.

Much to my dismay, Tammy kept opening the photo album from last year and pointing to decorating tricks we'd done. I pasted on a smile as she showed me pictures. Mitch was attentive in the meeting but didn't say much. I was sure that all the talk about decorations was out of his league. We all agreed to meet tomorrow before school started. I could hardly wait.

The meeting the next morning was just as painful as the first meeting. I tried shoving decisions off on Tammy and the girls, but they kept coming back to me for my opinions and ideas. I didn't care what size foil hearts we used; it didn't matter to me if the banners were white or pink. I didn't care if the punch was bright red or pink. I gave a huge sigh of relief when the bell rang and everyone had to leave.

"It will be a miracle if I make it through this dance," I said to Sally as we had lunch in my office. I set down my fork and explained how the high energy of the committee had me on the edge of tears, and how making conversation with Mitch was like talking to a dead man. "The girls want to talk about banners, garlands, balloons, colors, refreshments. Every time I see a heart I want to cry. I just wanted to ignore Valentine's Day."

"Well, you can't," Sally said. "It comes every year."

"I keep thinking of last Valentine's Day. I was so happy and in love, and then my life changed with one phone call."

"Bruce was a jerk," Sally said, "but you can't let him ruin Valentine's Day for you. Now is the time to put your painful memories away and start making new ones."

"That's easy for you to say. You've got a loyal husband who's taking you out for a lobster dinner on Valentine's Day."

"I think it's all in how you look at the holiday. We tend to think of Valentine's Day as a romantic day, but really it is a day to show love to everyone, not just those we're romantically interested in." She looked thoughtful for a moment and then continued. "You've got a perfect opportunity with the Sweetheart Dance. What better way to show love for the committee than to be excited about the dance—even if you don't feel like it."

"I know this dance means a lot to them, and much of the fun is actually putting the evening together." Pangs of guilt jabbed me. I knew I hadn't been as excited or warm about the dance as I should be.

"Then there's Mitch."

I rolled my eyes.

"From what you've told me about him, he must have been hurt by someone and he's still hurting."

"He's not much of a talker."

"So, you talk to him. When someone doesn't talk much it's easy to become non-talkative, too. Be your usual warm, outgoing self, even if he is standoffish or quiet. Maybe you'll burn through that cold exterior of his."

"What you're saying makes sense, but it's hard—"

24

"Of course it is. You've been hurt. But you're not going to get over your pain by carrying it with you. You'll only start feeling better as soon as you focus on other people, and not your pains from last year."

What she said made sense, from a logical viewpoint. Being excited about the dance and trying to talk to Mitch wouldn't be so easy with an aching heart. Tammy and her friends were so excited about the dance. They deserved a coordinator who was enthusiastic, too. As for Mitch, I'd try talking to him more and include him more often in the group conversations. I knew my strategies wouldn't be easy, but I'd try.

The next morning, I forced myself to be more interested in the garlands and hearts Tammy brought to the meeting. As usual, Mitch was sitting quietly. I couldn't think of a way to include him in the conversation. Colors and decorations weren't guy topics.

Tammy's eyes sparkled as she pulled out a piece of paper from her ring binder. It was a hand drawing of the backdrop she thought would look nice when the couples had their pictures taken. "I thought the suspended heart in the back would be neat," she said.

I studied the drawing. It was clever, but the school didn't have anything on hand to make it. "I'm not sure how we'd do that. What do you think, Mitch?"

Mitch leaned forward and I moved the drawing so he could see it better. "I could make a frame in my shop and we could hang a heart on it. We'd have to decorate the frame, and make the heart."

"That would work." Tammy's eyes gleamed as Mitch explained how he could make the backdrop. He grew more animated as he described the process and materials he could use. His eyes were a little brighter, and he even grinned as he joked about his supply of lumber.

The meeting was drawing to a close when Tammy turned her gaze toward me and grinned. "Are you bringing your husband this year? Her husband is so handsome," she said to everyone at the table.

My stomach twisted and my mouth went dry. I'd never told Tammy or the other students that I was divorced. It wasn't their business and it wouldn't make any difference to them.

"No, he won't be coming. We're divorced now."

"You're kidding!" Tammy's jaw dropped and her eyes were like saucers. "You were so perfect together. When did you break up?"

"We broke up shortly after the dance." Like, hours after the dance, I thought to myself. I rose from my chair, signaling the conversation was over, but Tammy continued on. "Who are you bringing to the dance?"

"I'm not bringing anyone this year. I'll be busy enough without entertaining a date." I walked toward the door.

"Mrs. Austin," Tammy called after me.

Why doesn't Tammy leave me alone? Before I could respond, Mitch called Tammy back to the table and asked her a question about her drawing. I knew he'd detained her so I could leave. That was nice of him. He was nice and helpful, even if he wasn't very friendly. Although I had seen small sparks of friendliness in him today that I hadn't seen before.

A couple of days later, I walked down to Mitch's classroom. I was going to use the backdrop as an excuse to drop in, but I really wanted to thank him for bailing me out of Tammy's endless questions at our last meeting. He was putting test tubes in a rack at one of the lab counters when I walked into the room. He looked up when I opened the door.

"Morning," he said.

"I came by to see how the backdrop is coming." I started to sit down on a lab stool, but he motioned me to come up to his desk.

"I've got some pictures I plan to show the committee." He pulled some photographs out of his desk drawer and handed them to me.

He'd done an excellent job of designing a frame. "This looks exactly like what Tammy had in mind."

"I showed her the pictures this morning and she was excited about it. Of course, she's got all kinds of ideas about decorating it." He smiled and laughed.

"I want to thank you for pulling Tammy back to talk to you the other day."

Mitch ran his hand through his hair and shook his head. "No problem. You did a great job of answering her questions. I'm sure it was painful for you."

I nodded.

"I can't imagine that you're happy to be coordinating the dance this year."

I was amazed at his sensitivity and perception about emotional pain. "I had some troubles at first, but things are getting better. It was time for me to move away from the past."

"Moving away from the past isn't easy." His eyes clouded. "Marie, my wife, died a couple years ago and I've had trouble getting through it."

"Is that her?" I turned toward the place on his desk where the picture stood. It wasn't there.

"Yes, she's the woman in the picture. I thought it was time to take the picture home."

I nodded and smiled. I knew it couldn't be easy for him to tell me these things about himself.

"Being assigned to the committee was the best thing that could've happened to me," he said. "I hadn't done any building projects since Marie died. I just wasn't in the mood. This backdrop got me back in

26

my shop, and I'm starting to feel better. I realized I'd been holding myself back from getting involved with life." He smiled warmly, and his eyes were filled with hope.

We continued talking until the morning bell rang and classes were starting. For a change, I hated to stop talking with him. As I walked back to the library, I replayed our conversation over and over in my mind. Mitch was quite a man. There was a lot to his personality once he opened up. He'd obviously suffered greatly with his wife's death. Sally had been right about him having some hurtful event behind his behavior. She and I would have to get rid of our nickname for him. Mr. Grumps didn't fit.

Sally was also right about my feeling better if I focused on the committee's needs rather than on my own feelings. Not that painful memories didn't sneak in and make my heart ache. But I was feeling a little better about Valentine's Day, even if it wouldn't be a romantic holiday for me. I'd joined the girls in their excitement, which was making the dance more fun for them and more pleasant for me. And maybe, just maybe, my question to Mitch about Tammy's drawing had helped him to take some steps to move away from his pain and on with his life.

At Sally's insistence, I bought a new dress for the dance. I was going to wear my favorite black dress, but she wouldn't hear of it. "You wear that everywhere!" she'd said. I didn't buy a red dress like last year. I bought a black silk dress to replace my old favorite.

I got to the school a couple of hours before the dance started. When I walked into the cafeteria, I stood at the door in awe of the room. I'd seen it only hours ago when we'd decorated. With the ladders gone and the lights dimmed, the room was magical. And romantic.

The kids will have a good time, I thought, as I headed to the kitchen to make punch.

"The room looks great, doesn't it?" Mitch said, coming up next to me. I'd thought he was good-looking before, but tonight he was handsome in his black suit. The scent of a fresh shower and musky cologne surrounded him and teased my nose.

"You did a wonderful job on the backdrop," I said. Maybe if I started talking I could ignore how his appearance made my heart beat erratically.

"All I did was nail some boards together. Tammy and her friends get all the credit for the finished product."

I ladled some punch into a cup and handed it to him. "What do you think?"

He took a sip and nodded his approval. "I have something for you." He handed me a small box that he'd set on the counter when he came in.

It was a florist box. Inside was a corsage of white carnations and

27

deep pink roses that created an intoxicating fragrance of sweetness and spice.

"For me?" I was puzzled. Why would he give me a corsage?

He nodded. His eyes met mine and he held my gaze.

"Thank you." I started to put it on, but my fingers were trembling.

"Let me help." His hand brushed mine as he lifted the corsage from my hands, sending warm chills through my veins.

I was all too aware of the warmth of his body as he touched me while he pinned the corsage to my dress. I told myself that the flowers had no romantic meaning. He was a nice man—he'd gotten me a corsage because he knew all the girls at the dance would have corsages.

I was having trouble dealing with this new Mitch. Mr. Grumps I could ignore, this man I couldn't. He stirred feelings in me that I thought were dead. He was not only physically attractive but he had a personality I liked more and more every time we were together.

As I expected, we had a large turnout for the dance. Judging from the smiling couples, the evening was a success. Mitch had to deal with a couple of boys who planned to spike the punch, and I dealt with smaller issues like broken shoe straps and zipper problems. When the dance was over my feet were killing me, and I was ready to fall into bed and sleep for hours. But Mitch and I had to take down the decorations so the cafeteria would be ready Monday morning.

I slipped off my high heels, Mitch took off his suit jacket and tie, and we began tearing down in an hour what had taken weeks to design. I was putting the last foil heart into a box when he came up to me.

"I think we're done." He gazed over the room that now looked too bright and all too much like a high school cafeteria.

"Thanks for all your help. I couldn't have done it without you." I slipped on my shoes.

"I know it's late, but would you like to get something to eat? I'm starved." His eyes looked boyish and his lips were curled into a shy smile.

"I'm hungry, too." My aching feet and tired body suddenly disappeared.

Since it was late, many places were already closed. We wound up at a pizza place that stayed open late. The restaurant was serving pizzas shaped like a heart, so we ordered one—it seemed appropriate for our late night meal. Over frosty mugs of beer and our pizza, we talked and talked. And made plans to see a movie the next day.

I learned a lesson this Valentine's Day about the power of love and putting my own pain aside to show love to others. I'm glad I made the effort to make the Sweetheart Dance a fun-filled, happy event. Little did I know that it would be a day I'd remember happily as well.

The End

CUPID SPEAKS ITALIAN
My Old World Mama Wouldn't Rest
Until She Found My Valentine!

I was of average height, slim, and freckle faced. I had red hair—not carrot red, but a bit darker—more like auburn. I was twenty-five years old when this story occurred.

My name is Giovanna Soprano. By the time I learned that my very Italian first name translates to Joan, it was too late; everyone called me Vanna.

I always argued with my Italian-immigrant parents about my name. I hated it; I wanted to be named Priscilla or Felicia or Daphne—these were beautiful, "Medigon" (American) names. But, no—my parents adhered to the old Italian tradition of naming the first baby girl after the paternal grandmother. It's a lucky thing for me that my grandmother wasn't named Eufemia or Immaculata! I used to beg and plead for them to take me to an attorney to have my name changed legally, but do you have any idea how stubborn and thickheaded an Italian father is? Think of the Rock of Gibraltar—and double it.

It was a lovely spring evening when I came home from work and Mamma greeted me in a very agitated manner. Mamma was a short, beautiful, vivacious brunette. I didn't take after her; I was calmer than she was but I had a bit of a temper, which I held in check as much as possible. I didn't want to be known as a bad-tempered Italian girl; I'd trained myself to be calm and serene—as much as I possibly could—and believe me, it was difficult. People always teased me about my freckles and hair.

As I said, Mamma was quite agitated that evening and I knew something was up. I immediately became alert because I knew this, whatever it was, involved me. A war was about to begin.

I have to explain that in Italian families, if all the sons but one are married, it's no cause for aggravation. But—and that's a big BUT—if one daughter has reached marriageable age and isn't married and has no prospects, the parents of this unfortunate creature become whacked out and they are beside themselves. They go to sleep and wake up to this horrible "problem" of an unmarried daughter; it seems to be a very shameful thing, indeed, to have an unmarried daughter who is older than twenty-one years of age. Prayers are said. Candles are lit. My parents thought I didn't know about all of the crazy things they did just so that God would send me a husband.

That evening, I looked at Mamma and she looked at me. She had

29

an expectant smile on her face and she was wringing her hands and then wiping them on her apron before she returned to wringing them again. This was a dead giveaway. Didn't she know by now that I always knew something was up when she acted that way?

"You know who call me today?" Mamma began. And without waiting for an answer, she continued, "Rosalie Nucherino, dats who."

I rolled my eyes to the ceiling, then to the window. I said, "Ma, who is Rosalie Nucherino and why should I even care who she is?"

"She the cousin of the cousin of you fadder. I no hear from her long time."

"Too bad, Ma. Who's the jerk she's promoting? And please explain 'the cousin of the cousin' part."

"Papa cousin, Caterina, her husband, Mario, his cousin, Graziella."

This didn't make sense to me but I was too annoyed and tired to start figuring it out so that it would make sense to me. "I don't want to meet him," I said. "I don't want to see him or hear any more about this whole thing." I was going to say "affair," but even though I knew Mamma didn't even know the definition of it, I decided to avoid that word.

"Why you talk like dat? You terrible. She call me cuz she want talk to me. Beh (well). She ask me 'bout you. I say you no marry and she say she know a nice boy no marry. You wanna know him?"

"Please, Ma. We've gone through all this a million times and I'm sick and tired of it. Your friends don't care what he looks like, what he does for a living. I mean, is he educated? Is he cultured? Is he a felon?"

"Oh, he a nice felon—a very nice felon. Very well educate and speak very well Italian."

I smiled at my mother's innocent funny. "Ma, does he have one ear higher than the other?" I asked sarcastically.

"Whatta you talk? He have ears like Papa. Why you talk like dis? You all the time talk fresh."

I started to get angry. "Ma, I don't want to meet any of the guys your friends recommend. They don't know what kind of life partner I'm looking for. Remember the guy Assunta sent here without telling me? I was never so humiliated in my life! He had no culture, no manners. He said he didn't like my freckles. He was illiterate."

"No," Mamma said, firmly shaking her head, "he no gotta literate. He very healthy. Rosalie say Carmine will call you tonight."

"Listen, Ma, I won't be home tonight. If he calls while I'm still here, tell him I'm not home. Please. You can tell a little lie for me, can't you? Huh? Okay? I'm going to my room now."

And I thought that would be the end of it.

Ah, stupid me. As though I didn't know Mamma.

Argument over, Mamma went to her stove full of pots. She was a superb cook. On Christmas Eve, when some Italians make it a point to cook seven different kinds of fish, Mamma cooked fish not so much by variety, as by the pound. Ton would be more like it. She would go to Passanisi's for fresh eels. Then to Gotti's for shellfish. By the time she finished cooking, she had platters of fried eel, fried silverfish, mussels in a thin tomato sauce, male crabs in another tomato sauce, clams, oysters, and what I called "pincushion fish," arranged temptingly on the long table.

Now, Mamma was a bit upset. Anyone who knew her well knew she was upset by the banging and clanging of her pots and pans. It sounded like the Triumphant March from Aida. Ah, what a beautiful opera!

I went to my little room. I changed my clothes and settled down on my bed to relax and catch up on a little reading before entering the kitchen for the second round. I knew Mamma would never let it be the end—and that I wasn't going to win.

Just as I was rising from my bed to go into the kitchen to set the table, my phone rang. I picked it up and just as I did so, I remembered "the call." My hand froze, poised a few inches above the cradle. What could I do? On the chance that it was Carmine, I certainly didn't want to give him the impression that I was just sitting by the phone, waiting breathlessly for his call. Slowly, I raised the phone to my ear with the intention of being as cruel and as smug as Joan Crawford. Surely, that would rid me of him for good.

"Hello?" I Crawforded.

"Hello," a soft, deep, melodic male voice said. "Is this Vanna?"

I'd never heard my dopey name spoken so seductively or beautifully. So huskily. Suddenly, it was a striking name—a name anyone would be proud of. Suddenly, I just loved it, and I made a mental note to thank my parents for giving me such a lovely name. I decided I would also apologize for being such a complainer all these years.

I could feel my mouth falling open. After a moment I sat up, alert, attentive . . . and suddenly very curious. "Yes, speaking."

"My name is Carmine Zanebono. We have a mutual friend, Rosalie Something-or-other, who told me a little about you. Anyway, you probably feel the same way I do about this sort of thing, and that's what I'm calling you to say, well . . . except that I'd like to hear your voice a bit more. Can you sing something for me?" He laughed.

Joan Crawford dematerialized. I came to. I laughed at his silly joke and we began talking. We talked and talked. And laughed. I thought, A sense of humor; very important.

We were still talking when Mamma knocked softly on my bedroom door. I looked toward the door; Mamma opened it just enough for her

31

to put her head in. When she saw me talking, she quickly closed the door. I rose and went to the door and opened it. She was in the hallway, talking to Papa, a big smile on her face as she spoke rapidly to him in Italian and gestured animatedly with her hands in that makeshift "sign language" that Italians are so adept at. Mamma threw kisses to heaven; she made the Sign of the Cross and whispered, "Grazie, Madonna!"

Papa, the poverino (poor guy), didn't know the entire story yet; he just suspected. But I'm sure Mamma filled him in, sotto voce. All Papa did was harrumph! He wanted to know more about this young man.

The next day, I told my friend, Gloria, about Carmine and his call. Gloria had been engaged and broken it and she was a bit cynical. She couldn't hold back her opinions and sometimes her opinions annoyed me. They annoyed me especially that day, because I liked Carmine and the sound of his voice, and Gloria told me in a very authoritative voice that he would not call back.

And he didn't.

Then I felt so bleak.

When Gloria asked me a week later if Carmine had called, I couldn't hide my disappointment. There was something in that young man's voice that had truly intrigued me. I knew he was sincere; I thought he was sincere. But suddenly, from his silence, I knew that he wasn't. But I was entranced, nonetheless. Enchanted. I was hooked. And his silence hurt me more than I dared admit.

Then he called me a few days later and asked if I would have dinner with him Saturday night. I accepted. Then I wondered if I'd accepted too quickly. I wanted to be worldly, after all; I didn't want to advertise my innocence. But I think it was written all over my freckled face.

Well, anyway, I had a date. I had to tell my parents that Carmine was coming to pick me up on Saturday. Naturally, Mamma went nuts. She cleaned the entire house. She made her very best pastries. I didn't know how to rein her in; she was like an Italian hurricane and tornado that had joined forces.

Saturday night came and I selected a blue dress—my favorite color and the color I looked best in. When the doorbell rang, it was Mamma who lost her head. She told Papa to sit down: "No, stand up! No—stand over there!"

I said in a stage whisper, "Ma, it's not the Pope coming—it's just Carmine Zanebono. Relax!"

How I wished I could heed my own advice. As it was, my heart was beating so fast—like sometimes your chest just throbs with every heartbeat, you know?

32

I opened the door. My mouth dropped open and instantly, I felt like a fool; how could I do that? Carmine Zanebono was supremely handsome.

Introductions were made. He'd brought me a small bouquet, which I took and thanked him. I excused myself and went into the kitchen to put the beautiful flowers in a vase. Mamma, in the meantime, asked him to sit down and served him wine and pastries. Carmine Zanebono was the perfect gentleman; he listened attentively to Mamma's eager small talk. She never let Papa have a chance to speak. Then I tried very gracefully to steer Carmine toward the door as I was getting more embarrassed by the minute.

We left, having said our good-byes to Mamma and Papa and when we got to his car parked out front, Carmine opened the door for me. On the drive to the restaurant, we made small talk and there were some awkward silences. I tried to think of clever things to say but I was suffering from brain freeze.

We went to a lovely restaurant; the atmosphere was excellent and the food was delicious. We got on beautifully once we were seated. Carmine made a few recommendations with regard to the menu and I allowed him to order for the two of us. We talked about our families, educations, our jobs, and ourselves. He apologized for not calling me sooner; he'd been sent out of town on business. At first, I didn't believe him; it sounded so implausible. He explained that he liked his job and there were times when he flew anywhere in the world to consult with other managers, supervisors, and even CEOs.

He was handsome and I was very aware of that. He had blue eyes, wavy hair, and the faintest hint of a cleft chin. He looked intently at me; I reddened. I was furious with myself. I was getting nervous and I have an annoying habit of twirling my already curly hair around my fingers when I get nervous. I stopped doing it when I realized he was watching me. I hoped I didn't have spinach stuck in my teeth— especially since neither of us had eaten spinach. The wine we drank with our dinner was making me feel warm all over and I hoped I wouldn't pass out on the floor right there. Sometimes I do goofy things.

He offered me more wine and I declined. I think he understood that I wasn't used to drinking wine. Even though we had wine at the dinner table every night, I wasn't much of a drinker. Wine made me sleepy so I generally avoided it, and I most certainly didn't want to be sleepy that night!

Afterward, when we left the restaurant, we drove through a dark, deserted stretch of road. He pulled over. He looked at me and I looked at him. I thought, Uh-oh. Now for the wrestling match. . . .

Slowly, he put his arms around me and pulled me close. I didn't

33

resist; I don't know why. It's almost as if I really didn't know what he was about to do. As though it had never happened to me before.

He kissed me—a long, sweet kiss. I was putty in his arms. He drew away for a moment and looked at me and then he started kissing me all over my face. It felt wonderful. Then he kissed me on my mouth—another lovely, lovely kiss. Then I felt his hands moving down from my shoulders and it was like an alarm went off inside of me. I pushed him away.

"No. Please—stop," I said quietly, but firmly.

He moved away from me. "I'm sorry," he said. "I didn't mean to disrespect you in any way or offend you. This is our first date and I'm behaving like an animal; I'm sorry. Please forgive me."

I wanted to say, "Oh, no—you're not an animal. I'm just a simpleton." But I didn't say a word. The words just stuck in my throat, which was beginning to hurt me from stress.

He reached over and tentatively took my hand in his. "I've been thinking about you ever since we talked on the phone. I had no idea what you looked like; people had told me you were 'beeooteefoo,' but you know how old Italians are. They always want to make a match and everyone is 'beeooteefoo.'"

He started the car and then we were moving again. I thought, I'm an idiot. I actually like this one and now, I'll never see him again! He's mad at me. He thinks I'm ugly. And I am! How stupid I am!

I was so absorbed in going over and over again with these miserable thoughts in my mind that I didn't even realize I was crying. Then we were home—parked in front of my house. He came around and opened the door for me. I couldn't even look at him, I was so embarrassed. I wished I could disappear or evaporate. Then we were at the door and he took out his clean handkerchief and wiped away the tears on my cheeks; I hadn't even realized they were there.

He put his hand out for my key. After he'd unlocked the door for me, he handed it back to me. Then he took me in his arms, looked at me, and kissed me for a long, long time. It felt so good, so natural for me to be in his arms and for him to be kissing me and for me to be kissing him back. He gave me another long kiss before he finally, hesitantly, drew away.

"Goodnight, Vanna," he said softly, tenderly. And he turned and started to walk away.

I thought, I'll never, never see him again. I was certain it'd been his farewell kiss. The kiss of death for me.

He stopped, turned back to face me, and smiled before exclaiming, "I'm going to marry you!"

The End

VALENTINE FROM
MY DAUGHTER
She Set Me Up With My Dream Man!

I sat in the kitchen, reflecting on the phone conversation I had with my daughter, Kathleen, wishing my life could be a little brighter. Since I had been widowed, I had no idea what to do with myself.

When the doorbell rang and jolted me from my thoughts, I was totally unprepared for what I saw. Standing on my front porch was the most handsome middle-aged man I'd ever laid eyes on. Suddenly, I felt self-conscious because I'd answered the door without bothering to check myself in the mirror.

"Gretchen Robertson?" he said.

I had no idea who this man was, but I nodded. "Yes, that's me."

He glanced at a sheet of paper he was holding, and then he narrowed his eyes as he looked me in the eye. "A woman by the name of Kathleen Moll told me you needed some work done, and I'm here to take care of it."

I blinked as I realized my daughter had called this man. With a forced chuckle, I shook my head. "Kathleen Moll is my daughter. I mentioned to her that I'd like a few things done around here, but I don't think I can do it yet."

What I didn't tell the man was that I was flat broke after fixing the leak in the bathroom. Anything else I had done would have to wait until my next check from my deceased husband's company arrived.

The man extended his hand and introduced himself. "My name is Frank Barrymore. I'm a carpenter, but I can do other things, too."

"I'm sorry," I said. "Maybe some other time."

"She called me and said not to take 'no' for an answer." He'd quit looking at his paper and was now looking at me again. Now I saw amusement in his eyes. He looked harmless.

I took a step back and invited him in. "Why don't you come on in and let me call her?" I said. "Would you care for some coffee?"

"Sure," he said. "I drink mine black."

I poured the man some coffee and asked him to take a seat in the kitchen while I walked back to my room, where I placed a call to Kathleen's office. "What's this man doing here?" I asked. "He says you told him I needed some things done around the house."

"Mom, this is from Nick and me," she explained. "Please take this gift. It's so hard to know what to buy you, and we figured you'd like

35

something you could use more than jewelry or knickknacks."

Kathleen was right, as usual. For a twenty-something young woman, my daughter sure was wise. She'd been married for three years to the guy she'd gone with since high school, and they'd looked after me since my husband, Kirk, had died.

"Okay," I finally conceded. "I'll let this guy do a couple of things, but I don't want you to go overboard. After all, you're not made of money."

Kathleen laughed. "Mom, you're impossible. Nick and I are doing just fine financially, and this was his suggestion."

"But Kathleen—" I said before she interrupted.

"Mom, Nick and I appreciate all the things you did for us when we first got married. You and Dad even helped with the down payment on our house, for heaven's sake."

"I know, but you're my daughter," I argued.

"And you're my mother, so let us do this." Her tone was firm and commanding.

When I got off the phone, I returned to the kitchen and looked at Frank. "I spoke with my daughter, and she insisted I accept this gift from her. When do you want to start?"

"How about today?" he asked.

With a shrug, I replied, "Sure." I had to stop and think about what was the most important thing that needed work. There were so many problems with my house that I wasn't sure what he should do first. I looked at him helplessly and smiled. His expression was very tender and understanding, which made me feel more comfortable about having him here.

"Why don't we make a list, and I'll take a look and see what's the most urgent?" he suggested.

"Okay," I said.

We sat at the kitchen table and I told him everything I could think of while we drank coffee. Then we got up and walked through the house, where he noticed even more repairs that needed to be done.

I sighed. "I don't want to take advantage of my daughter's generosity," I said.

"Hey, don't worry about it. I'm giving her a price break on materials and a great deal on labor."

"Thanks, Frank. Let me know if you need anything." Our gazes locked and my heart fluttered. I had to force myself to look away.

I left him alone to get started on what he considered the most urgent of repairs. When noon drew near, I asked if he'd like to join me for soup and a sandwich. He said he'd be delighted.

As we ate, I found myself laughing for the first time in a very long time. Frank was such a fun man to chat with. Finally, he stood up, folded his napkin, and carried his dishes to the sink. "I need to get back to work, Gretchen. Thanks for lunch."

All afternoon, I busied myself in the house, trying my best to catch a glimpse of Frank as he worked without him noticing what I was doing. A couple of times, he turned around and winked. I felt my face grow hot. Imagine that—blushing at my age.

It was nearly dark out when he came to me and said he was quitting for the day. "I'll be back tomorrow for the next round of repairs," he told me.

"Oh, you don't have to come back," I said. "All the important things have been fixed." Deep down, I wanted to see him again, to have this man in my house, but I didn't want to take advantage of him or my daughter and her husband.

He tilted his head forward and gave me a long look that made my knees go weak. "It's all important to me, Gretchen. I don't like anything to be broken."

I gulped. The man was absolutely great looking, and he exuded a sensuality that I'd never seen before in my life. Since I'd been rendered speechless, all I could do was nod.

That night, I lay in bed staring up at the ceiling, thinking about Frank. It had been a very long time since I'd looked at a man and thought of things that had crossed my mind with Frank. After Kirk had died, I thought I'd never meet a man who affected me that way.

The next morning, in spite of the fact that I hadn't gotten much sleep, I woke up before the sun came up. First thing I did was make a pot of coffee, and then I showered. As soon as I thought my daughter might be awake, I dialed her number.

"Hey, Mom," she said. "How's Frank working out?" Her voice was light, and she sounded very pleased with herself.

"Great. He's coming back today. Kathleen, honey, you don't have to do this."

"Wait a minute," my daughter said. "We hired him to come over for a day. Are you sure he said he's coming back today?"

Right then, the doorbell rang. I leaned off to the side and glanced out the window. "Yes, that's him right now. I see his truck in the driveway."

Kathleen sighed. "He must be slower than I thought. Either that, or Nick told him to work until everything was done, no matter how long it takes."

I got off the phone and hurried to answer the door. Before Frank came inside, I asked about arrangements to come back the second day.

With a wide grin, he said, "They hired me to come yesterday. Today is a bonus."

"Bonus?" I asked.

Frank nodded and grinned. "I enjoyed being here so much yesterday, I figured I'd come back today. Besides, I know you're a sweet, caring woman, and you won't let me go hungry." He gave me a mock puppy-dog look that made me laugh.

I nodded. "Okay, then, come on in. I'll fix a big lunch since I can't afford to pay for everything you're doing."

"Food's better than money any day."

All morning, I worked on fixing a huge meal. I cooked chicken, seasoned mashed potatoes, Southern-style green beans, and cornbread. He walked into the kitchen, sniffing the air. "Smells great," he said. "What time is lunch being served?"

I held my hands out to my side. "Whenever you're ready to take a break."

"How about now?"

I loved his eagerness. It had been a long time since I'd prepared a meal for a man, and I'd forgotten what it felt like. Doing this made me feel important and appreciated. "Have a seat," I said as I lifted a potholder and opened the oven door.

We had a wonderful talk over a two-hour lunch. He asked me all kinds of questions about my family, and I told him I'd been alone since Kirk had died two years ago. He said he'd been divorced for five years, and he hadn't had a serious relationship since then. His children were grown and lived in other states, so he lived alone in an apartment until he figured out what to do next. After his early retirement, he'd done some fishing and played golf, but he soon grew tired of not working. That was when he began to hire himself out as a handyman.

"I'm glad," I said. "Otherwise, everything in my house would be broken forever."

"Oh, I'm sure some nice man would've come along eventually." He smiled at me and winked.

Once again, I was flustered, but I managed to smile back. "Maybe."

After he ate his dessert, he said he only had a few things left to do, and then he'd be finished. My heart fell with a thud at the thought of Frank not coming back.

All afternoon, I tried to think of a way to get him back. He beat me to the punch, though, by giving me a business card and saying that he'd be glad to come back if anything else broke down.

He grinned at me and added, "I work for food, too. Since I have a nest egg and a retirement check coming in every month, I don't need your money."

After Frank left, I kept looking for things to break down, but nothing ever did. He'd done such a good job of fixing things; everything in my house was in great working order.

38

Kathleen and Nick came over and inspected his work. "Mom, he's really good, isn't he?" my daughter said.

I nodded then turned away, hoping she wouldn't see my expression. She didn't, but Nick did.

"Gretchen," he said in a teasing manner, "you like Frank, don't you?"

I self-consciously lifted my hand to pat my hair down like I did when I was nervous. "Yes, he's a very nice man."

Kathleen gasped. "Mom, you really do like Frank, don't you?"

"Of course, honey, I just said I did." It was very hard for me to share this kind of feeling with my daughter, but I didn't want to lie.

"No, I mean really, really like him." Her eyes were wide with amazement.

I let out a sigh. "Okay, yes, I really, really like him."

Nick chuckled. "I should have known something like this would happen."

Turning to Kathleen, I said, "Does it bother you that I'm attracted to a man?"

"Not really. If you'd been attracted to anyone right after Dad died it would've bothered me, but it's been a long time, and you're a very pretty, smart, loving woman."

Still smiling, Nick nodded. "Kathleen definitely has your looks, Gretchen."

My eyes teared over at their sweet compliments. "I love you both."

"And we love you, too," they both said at the same time.

I saw them exchange a glance, but I didn't think anything of it. Nick told Kathleen to get their coats, and he'd be with her in a minute. As soon as she left me alone with her husband, he turned to me.

"I've been having a hard time figuring out what to do for Kathleen for Valentine's Day. Can you give me some ideas?"

"Sure," I said. "I'll call you at work next week."

"I really appreciate it," he said as he edged toward the door. "Just don't let Kathleen know how inept I am in the romance department."

Now it was my turn to laugh. "You're not inept, Nick. In fact, you're a very smart man for asking in advance. It shows you're thinking of her."

He leaned over and kissed me on the cheek before they left. I felt so blessed that my daughter had such a great husband who was willing to go to the trouble of being nice to me. At least I wasn't completely alone in the world.

If only I had a man to love me, I thought later on that night. Even though I had my daughter and son-in-law nearby, I still spent the nights alone in my big bed. My heart ached for the tenderness and loving touches in a committed relationship.

As I promised, I called Nick at his office the next week. "I have a few ideas of things you can do for Kathleen for Valentine's Day."

"Okay, start talking. I'll write as you tell me."

I gave him a list of a half dozen ideas, from sending her flowers to kidnapping her from her office to take her to a surprise dinner. She wasn't that interested in candy, but she loved fine dining, just like I did.

"Thanks, Gretchen," he said. "Kathleen loves the element of surprise."

"So do I," I told him.

He hesitated before telling me good-bye. When I got off the phone, I sank down in the kitchen chair and thought about how Kirk used to surprise me. One of my favorite Valentine's Day surprises had been on a Saturday when he'd blindfolded me and taken me on a picnic by a waterfall. He'd even gone to the trouble to set up a table in advance, complete with flowers and white tablecloth. My relationship with my husband had been very romantic, until the very end.

Frank dropped by one afternoon on his way home from a job and asked how everything was going. I told him all the things he'd fixed were still in great shape. He chuckled. "I was hoping something else was broken."

My heart was broken, but I couldn't tell him that. "You did a wonderful job."

He stood and looked at me for a long moment before he began to back away. "I guess I need to go now," he said awkwardly. "I just wanted to stop by and make sure about everything."

He was almost to his car when I held up my hand. "Frank! Wait."

Frank paused and lifted his eyebrows. "You need something?"

"I was wondering if you'd like to come over for lunch tomorrow."

His expression changed from frustration to happiness. "Sure, I'd love it. What time?"

"Noon?"

"I'll be here."

Over lunch the next day, Frank and I had a wonderful talk, but he had to go back to his job. "I'll get in touch with you soon, Gretchen. Thanks so much for lunch."

"It was my pleasure," I told him, and I meant it.

A couple of weeks went by, and I hadn't heard from him, so I figured he'd moved on or been too busy to think about me. Loneliness replaced hopefulness, and I was worse off than before I met Frank.

Valentine's Day arrived, bringing my old memories crashing into my mind. This was one of the most difficult days I had to face each year.

With a sigh, I figured I'd never have another Valentine's Day like those I shared with Kirk again. At least I had my memories to carry me through the day, although I knew some of them would make me cry.

That morning, Kathleen called me. "Hi, Mom!" she said with enthusiasm. "Happy Valentine's Day."

"Same to you, sweetie," I told her. I had to fight to hold back the tears. Today was certain to be the worst Valentine's Day ever, as the loneliness was beginning to overwhelm me. My first Valentine's Day without my husband had been difficult, but I was still numb from the shock of losing him at such a young age. Now, I was fully aware of everything around me, and it seemed as if I was the only person I knew not part of a couple.

"Mind if I stop by for lunch?" she asked.

"That would be great," I told her. I meant it, too. "What would you like me to fix?"

"Nothing. I'm bringing lunch."

"You don't have to do that, Kathleen," I informed her. "I can have something ready for you when you stop by."

"No," she insisted. "I'll bring something, and I won't take no for an answer. It's Valentine's Day."

I chuckled. "Well, in that case, who am I to argue?"

At least I wouldn't be alone all day. Since I figured Kathleen was going to a lot of trouble for me today, I decided to take a long bath and put on some decent clothes.

She arrived with her arms full of things from the deli and bakery close to where she worked. "I've got an extra hour, so we can relax for a little while," she said as she carried everything inside and set it on the table.

I thoroughly enjoyed having lunch with Kathleen. The food was good, but the company was excellent. In fact, I actually forgot to feel sorry for myself until after she went back to her office. She'd asked me a bunch of questions about whether or not I had plans for the night, but after I answered her, she quickly changed the subject. We laughed and talked like a couple of girlfriends until she left.

Then the loneliness crept in again. I sat and stared at the wall of family pictures as memories of my wonderful marriage passed through my mind. Kirk was a great husband, even after his death, when he left me this house fully paid for and a small pension signed over to me so I wouldn't have to go back to work until I wanted to. I guess I should have stopped thinking about being alone and focused on the positive of how fortunate I was for having had a wonderful marriage. But it was hard.

As the afternoon passed, I wandered around the house, trying to think of something to do to occupy my mind until this day for lovers was over. When I turned on the TV, all they talked about was romantic things to do with your mate. I quickly flipped it off and picked up the latest women's magazine I subscribed to. Even that was filled with ideas for a romance-filled day of love. Finally, I decided to listen to some old CDs and work on some needlepoint. I laughed at myself as I thought about how my grandmother used to do this. I never imagined myself sitting in a rocking chair, doing needlework at such a young age, but here I was.

The afternoon dragged by, but finally, it was time to start thinking about what I was going to do for dinner. I hadn't done anything active all day, so I wasn't very hungry.

Then the doorbell rang. I sat in the chair for a couple of seconds, wondering who in the world would've stopped by unannounced. Kathleen had already paid me a visit, and all my friends had plans. Oh well, it was probably just a door-to-door salesman. I decided I might as well be nice to him since he obviously didn't have anyplace to go today, either.

Imagine my surprise when I opened the door to find Frank standing there in front of me, holding a single red rose, dressed in a suit. "Hi, Gretchen," he said. "I hope you're alone."

"Uh, yes, I'm alone," I said as I backed away from the door.

He thrust the rose toward me. "Happy Valentine's Day, Gretchen."

I took the rose and passed it beneath my nose. It was fragrant and very beautiful. "Thank you, Frank," I said. "This is very sweet."

He raised his eyebrows. "Sweet? If you say so." He glanced around behind me and then looked me in the eye. "I hope you don't mind, but I spoke to your daughter and asked if she thought you had plans for tonight."

"Oh?" I said. "And what did my daughter say?"

"She said if I hurried up and didn't waste any time, you might still be available."

"Kathleen said that?" I asked, amused at his choice of words.

Frank nodded. "Yes, and she also thought you might like to go out to dinner and to a show."

"When did you speak to my daughter?" I asked.

"Early this morning. I called to talk to Nick, but he'd already gone to work."

So Kathleen knew about this when she came over for lunch. I wondered why she'd been so nosy about my plans for the night. Now I understood.

"So, how are all the repairs holding up?" Frank asked, as he obviously tried to cover for the awkwardness of the moment.

"So far, so good," I said. "In fact, I think you fixed some things better than new."

42

He looked down at me and my heart did a double-flip. "Well?" he asked. "Would you like to go out with me tonight, or am I just making a fool of myself?"

Suddenly, I felt more at ease than I'd felt in a long time. I eagerly nodded. "I'd love to go out with you, Frank. I hope you don't mind waiting a few minutes for me to change into something more appropriate for the occasion."

He beamed at me. "I'll wait here. Take your time."

As soon as I had the rose in a vase of water, I quickly went to my room and changed into my prettiest red dress. I reapplied my makeup that had worn off after a few tears had escaped during the afternoon, and then I brushed my hair to a high shine. I decided to wear it down, since Kathleen told me once it made me look younger and more feminine.

My heart fluttered as Frank looked at me with open admiration. "Ready?" he said as he stood.

"As ready as I'll ever be." And I meant it, too. It was about time I got out and started living again.

Frank was very sensitive about this being the first time I'd been out with a man since my husband died. Apparently, Kathleen filled him in on how depressed I'd been. He asked all the right questions and took cues from me on what to say next. I appreciated his sensitivity.

We had dinner at a fabulous Italian restaurant, and then he suggested a show. I had a great time laughing and talking with Frank, and he seemed to enjoy himself as well. When it was time for him to take me home, I had a feeling I'd see him again.

He kissed me on the cheek and said good night, asking if he could call me again. When I floated inside the house, I saw the light blinking on my answering machine. Kathleen's message was filled with hope as she asked me to call her as soon as I got home.

"Well?" she said the second she picked up the phone. She obviously knew it was me.

"Thanks, Kathleen," I said.

There was a long pause. "Thanks in a good way?" she asked. "Or are you being sarcastic?"

"It's better than a good way. I had a great time with Frank."

My daughter let out a sigh of relief. "I was worried. Nick said he was sure you liked Frank, but I was sort of doubtful."

"Tell me about your Valentine's Day," I said, hoping to redirect the conversation. It was sort of embarrassing discussing my love life with my daughter.

Kathleen went on and on about how romantic Nick had been. "He had flowers delivered to my office, Mom. You wouldn't believe how big the arrangement was. Everyone was envious. And then he came to my office and told me he had a big surprise and to close my eyes. You wouldn't believe what he did."

I laughed. Nick was an excellent student in matters of the heart. I was flattered that he'd listened to me and taken my advice. "Tell me."

"He hired a limo to take us to the best restaurant I've ever been to in my life." Then she told me about how dreamy everything was and how he'd never be able to top that.

"But he'll have fun trying, I'm sure," I said.

"You're still not off the hook, Mom," she said.

"What do you mean by that?" I asked.

With a low chuckle, she said, "Nick said Frank wants to start seeing more of you. He really likes you, Mom."

So much for not discussing my love life with my daughter. "I like him, too."

That was a year ago. Frank stopped by again two days later and asked if I'd like to see a movie. We started going out regularly after that. Once in a while he lets me cook a meal for him, but he says he wants to pamper me and give me a break from routine. He's such a sweetheart.

I have a feeling he has big plans for this Valentine's Day. Kathleen and Nick have been hanging around, asking questions about my feelings for Frank, and looking at me funny. Frank has dropped hints that he's starting to think about the future and I'm in all his plans. Kathleen has already let me know that she thinks Frank and I make a "darling couple." I laugh at her choice of words, but I agree.

Hopefully, Frank will have a black velvet box in his pocket, but even if he doesn't, I know he'll continue to be a very important part of my life. I thoroughly enjoy being around him, and he lets me know all the time how much he likes being with me.

My daughter had no idea when she and Nick hired a handyman to fix things in my house that they were also mending my heart. Even though Kathleen didn't realize it at the time, she'd given me the best Valentine's Day gift of all—hope for the future with a wonderful man.

The End

THE VALENTINE'S DAY CLUB
We Make Sure Nobody Gets Left Out–
No Matter How Lonely-Hearted!

I get good and mad on Valentine's Day—the kind of anger that tears from your soul, ripples through your heart, and quakes your body enough to wrench the tears from your eyes.

Mind you—I'm very happily married to a good ol' Southern man who graciously presents me with a bouquet of flowers and a box of chocolates in good manner each year. Still, the holiday always presents a sort of forlorn angst as I look around at the souls who no longer stand in the position that I do.

No other holiday seems as exclusionary to me. At Christmastime, no matter what your religious beliefs, there's still a loophole in the holiday with Santa and his merry elves, sparkling lights, and goodwill toward man. Even if you choose to not imbibe in the holiday spirit at all, there are some killer bargains to be found in the shopping malls. Something for everyone.

Valentine's Day is just not so. As a noteworthy day for lovers, it bears with it a prerequisite of having that significant other to celebrate with, lest you're resigned to sending quirky cards to your relatives and closest friends while burying yourself in a cocoon of chocolate and, often, despair. I dwelled in this Valentine's Day hole for the better part of my youth before I emerged from the chrysalis when I met Warren at the age of twenty-six.

With a partner, the holiday took on a new light. No longer subject to scarfing down burgers and fries from the local fast-food joint, I was able to dine in glory on February fourteenth with my beau. A whole new world of cards, treats, and presents spread before me and for the first year or so, I admit I danced with glee to be a member of the Valentine's Day "in" club.

Then I got mad.

The anger came upon me slowly, drawing me in a little at a time with each passing year. There were many events that triggered my downfall. As I first recall, it started around 1977 when I realized that my dearest friend, Cathy, who was usually between boyfriends, grew sullen each February and seemed to vanish until the dreaded holiday passed. Then there were other dark moments: The time Betsy skipped around the office in anticipation, only to be found hours later crying in her cubicle the next day as her boyfriend failed to live up to her expectations and showed up sans gift on that important night, and just a year ago, when dear Cathy celebrated her first Valentine's Day as a widow—alone in her newly purchased condo.

I should've invited her to join Warren and I. I should've called her daughter to encourage her to stop by for a visit. Shoulda, coulda—didn't. My anger and angst over the holiday clouded my better judgment.

Fortunately, I had a year's time to chastise myself good and hard. I also had a year to devise a plan.

As my fifty-fifth Valentine's Day approached, a sly smile stuck on my lips and a bubble of euphoria followed my trail. Even Warren commented on my upbeat demeanor, which was an unexpected, and, most likely, delightful change for him after all these years. What could I do but give the big lug a hug and clue him in. Warren's encouragement sealed the deal and I pressed forward with my elaborate plan.

Fortunately, the holiday fell on a Saturday, which would give me a greater amount of time to carry out my idea. The first time might be a little rough and I was unable to foretell personal reactions.

Morning rose and I scurried around the house, assembling every last detail, pausing to check things off as I went along in a notebook where I'd also listed other objectives for the day in an orderly fashion. A consummate organizer, my Type A personality often serves me well. That day was no exception.

What that orderly personality couldn't dissuade, though, was the rapid beat of my heart and the giddy air of anticipation, which seemed to cling to the walls of my home and formed a parade of their own. If I'd dared to step outside the house, I imagined I might find balloons and confetti springing up the chimney from the well of jubilation inside.

The doorbell rang at precisely ten o'clock that morning. Warren jumped off his comfortable position on the couch to answer it before I could respond from my encampment in the dining room. I suspected that my enthusiasm even snuck into his tired-of-my-wife-getting-angry-every-Valentine's-Day bones.

Much to my delight, my best, friend, Cathy walked in, offered Warren a quick hug, and then approached me with a quizzical look on her face as Warren closed the front door behind her.

She didn't even wait for our customary greeting before her words pounded the air. "Okay, Audrey. The gig is up; now spill. What have you been up to?"

The smile on my face probably rivaled the one from the day I married. "Come in the dining room and I'll be happy to explain."

We embraced and then I led her toward the dining room table I'd spent the morning preparing. She tilted her head and scanned the assortment of hors d'oeuvres mixed with what resembled the contents of a middle school teacher's art cabinet.

Cathy dropped her arm from mine. "What on earth?"

A small titter escaped my lips. "Interesting assortment, huh?"

"I'd say. Now are you going to clue me in?"

"Have a seat and I'll fill in all the details."

Warren interrupted for a moment to cordially offer to bring our guest a drink, and then disappeared into the kitchen. Cathy and I sat down, angled from each other by the corner of the table.

As glad as a person could be that Cathy would be the first inductee into my plan, I took a deep breath and began. "You know how Valentine's Day has always pained me for a variety of reasons?" A nod of her head urged my continuation. "Well, I got a bee in my bonnet this year and decided to dust off old habits and let go of some of that nonsensical rage."

"That's great to hear, but that still doesn't explain..." Cathy waved her hand at the colorful collection of items strewn across the dining room table.

"I'm getting there. You see, what I've always hated the most about this day is the narrow view which permeates it from the time we realize the distinguishing characteristics of the opposite sex."

"You're losing me a bit here. Run that by me again."

Warren entered the room with two glasses of sweet tea in hand. "Honey, just what are these distinguishing characteristics you all are speaking about?"

"William, not now." Normally I might have indulged him or offered a laugh, but my husband's penchant for silly innuendos ran far from the serious nature of my big idea on the table, so to speak. "Okay, what I mean is, remember when we were very little, we passed paper Valentines to everyone in school, made cards for family, friends, and even the pastor and the neighbors? We didn't discriminate or even realize that the day stood for more than hearts and modest expressions of love until years later. I realized that's when I began this innate hatred of the holiday. So this year—" the words raced from me as the first light of understanding flickered in Cathy's eyes, "—I decided, to heck with tradition. I wanted to go back to kindergarten, to the time where Valentine's Day stood for one thing only."

"Love." Cathy breathed the word and it seemed to swirl around us. Tears beaded in the corner of her eyes.

I placed my hand in hers. "Yes. So from this year forward, I decided my Valentine's Days would be about holding on to that innocent notion. I decided to start, well, a Valentine's Day Club. You know, sort of like the Red Hats, but only once a year. Well, really not like them as we're meeting for the sole purpose of creating handmade Valentines, but you get the picture."

47

Tears flowed down Cathy's face freely, mixed with a loopy grin and a rush of laughter.

If that didn't put a thorn in my finger. I looked to Warren for support, but the doorbell rang and he rushed off to answer it.

I shifted in my chair, seemingly unable to find a comfortable spot. "What's so funny? Do you think it's dumb? I surely didn't mean to upset you." I was at a loss with no idea how to interpret her bizarre reaction.

She wiped her eyes with the edge of her knuckles and the laughter tapered off to a soft giggle. "Heavens no, Audrey. I'm happy as mouse in a cheese factory that you've finally come to your senses! I thought you had this elaborate scheme to try and bail me out from a lonely holiday without Hank, and I've never been gladder to be wrong. The Valentine's Day Club is a splendid idea!"

I heaved a sigh of relief, promptly followed by a series of giggles. "Thank the good Lord!"

"So, why don't you fill me in on what all you've dreamed up here."

"While you're at it, Mom," my daughter's voice streamed in from the doorway, "fill us in, too."

I jumped up to hug her and her husband and usher them in. Warren gave me a wink and headed back to the front door as the doorbell chimed again.

As my family and closest friends piled in, I explained the basic gist of the plan. We were to design and decorate as many Valentine's Day cards as we possibly could in a two- to three-hour period while feasting on the array of goodies I'd spread out, as well as enjoy each other's company. Our first objective was to make cards for our inner circles of friends, neighbors, and relatives of our choosing, then we'd each tackle a list of a few special recipients I'd come up with—including the workers and residents of the assisted living community my mother stayed at and the local postal workers who carried their extra weight this time of year.

The afternoon would be spent delivering our cards and after, those who wished to would meet back at my house for festive dinner. Next year, I explained, we could add to the list and spread out the simple message of the holiday farther.

Everyone got gung-ho and dove into creating cards ranging from spectacular works of art to simplistic, but lovely, greetings. We labeled each with care, shared ideas, and shared our lives around that table filled with hearts. Each one of us pledged to continue the tradition into the future and meet up each year, even if we had to host the card-building activities the night before the holiday to ensure proper deliveries on the big day.

I spent a long time being mad at a holiday when my energy

could've been spent celebrating the true nature of love. After all, who dictated that the holiday of lovers ritually excludes all the loved ones in our lives? Maybe the restaurant specials or the prime marketing forces don't target the various relationships of love, but that didn't mean that I had to stand for it or refuse to recognize the opportunity I was granted to find a new way of embracing the holiday by returning to the teachings of my youth.

I'm now a proud member of the Valentine's Day Club and looking forward to expanding our recipient and membership circles—one love at a time.

The End

LOVE IN THE BIG EASY
I Found Romance And More At Mardi Gras

That night had been perfect. Craig and I moved among our friends and family, holding flutes of congratulatory champagne and each other's hands. The small private dining room was the same where our rehearsal dinner would be held. Our wedding date had been set for Valentine's Day, right after Craig completed his six-month job transfer to England.

I met Craig Corning when my family moved from our very small town to one slightly larger. It was hard to start over in a new high school in my junior year, but Craig and his sister made the transition so much better than it could have been. Our families were close, and they literally leaned across the fence that separated our yards to share a cup of coffee, borrow a cup of sugar, and talk about the day's events. According to some, the Corning siblings' roles were switched: auburn-haired Abby was a jock, lettering in lacrosse and basketball, while dark blonde Craig was a certified geek—whose advanced placement classes earned him college credit even before he graduated from high school.

When we graduated, Craig went to Boston to attend college, while I attended a state school an hour away. We still saw each other at Christmas and breaks from school, but nothing clicked until the summer after we both graduated from college.

We were sitting out in his parents' backyard. It was a perfect summer night—not too hot, not too humid. Stars and fireflies were out. The night was like a commercial for the perfection of summer. Somehow, our hands touched, and then our lips. Craig and I went on our first real date a week later; and as the saying goes, the rest is history. I thought my future was secure until a couple of days after the party.

I attributed his lack of enthusiasm to jet lag and becoming re-acclimated to life at home. We were sitting on the porch of the little cottage I had purchased a couple of years ago before I knew that I would be Mrs. Craig Corning.

"What's the matter?" I smiled over at him. "Jet lag? Too many gushing relatives?"

Craig turned to give me a small smile. "No, it's nothing like that." He sat forward, looking absolutely pained. "Lauren, we need to talk." I felt my stomach clench. That look and those words did not bode well.

He grabbed my hands, although that was not all comforting.

50

"No, I think you need to talk. Go ahead; don't leave me sitting here to wonder what you have to tell me."

"I have loved you for a long time."

Uh-oh, here comes the kiss-off. There was nothing at all amusing about what I knew was going to happen, but it helped to keep my emotions under control.

"But when I went to England, I realized that I hadn't been anywhere or experienced life outside of home and Boston, and maybe, sometimes New York. All of a sudden, I began to feel confined."

"By me? By the idea of our marriage?"

Craig shook his head.

"No, not you, specifically. I love you, but I'm not in love with you. I would have been happy to be married to you, until I spent time in Europe. I realized I was settling for what was comfortable and familiar—rather than just putting myself out there to experience more of life."

I was already devastated, but the word "settling" made me angry. I jumped up from my seat. My first were balled so tight, my nails dug into my palms.

"So you're saying that marriage to me would be settling?"

Craig jumped up to face me. I could see he was torn by what he wanted and hurting me.

"No, no, that's not what I mean. I mean that in the end, I wouldn't be the best husband for you. Not the other way around."

We waited for two days to pass before we broke the news to our parents. There was some tension between them for a while, and that made both of us sad. Both of us talked to our mother and father. I took mine aside.

"Look, whatever happened or didn't happen with me and Craig, it has nothing to do with Mr. & Mrs. Corning. They were just as upset and surprised as you two. Please don't let this turn into some kind of Hatfield and McCoy feud."

Instead of sticking around so close to the scene of the crime, Craig made plans to take a vacation out on the West Coast.

"I need some time away from the turmoil caused by my decision," he told me. "And then, I need to figure out exactly where I'm headed."

That was nine months ago. It took me some time to get over the fact that I wouldn't be a bride. For a while, I felt stood up at the altar, but thankfully, it hadn't gotten that far. At least, we didn't have to return a boatload of wedding gifts. I could laugh about it, now. Looking back, I realize know that Craig was right. Our marriage wouldn't have exploded; it would have slowly unraveled and died a slow and painful death!

The date we had set for our wedding was coming up. Even though

I had come to terms with our break-up, I knew that date would be difficult for me. I needed something that would lift my spirits. I didn't want to reflect, I wanted to have fun. My friend, Janet, and I booked tickets for New Orleans Mardi Gras; but at the last minute, she had to back out.

"Lauren, you can't go to a place like that by yourself, especially during Mardi Gras. There'll be a whole of drunken people out on the streets, behaving badly, picking pockets, and who knows what else. That 's not the place for a woman alone."

My mother tugged on the cord she used to keep from losing her glasses.

I turned to my father.

"Go ahead, I know you have something to say, also."

My dad shook his head,

"Not me, sweetheart. You're grown, you've made up your mind, and you need some fun. Just keep your cell phone charged, and stay in contact with us. Leave us the name of your hotel, and everything will be fine." He drew me close for a hug. "I know it will."

"At least, I can drive you to the airport," Janet told me. When she left me at the curb with my bag, she leaned out of the window with a wicked grin. "Keep your shirt down. I don't want to see your boobs on the news!"

I could feel the festive air as soon as I got off the plane. I didn't have any trouble getting a cab to my hotel near the French Quarter. I had never seen so many people in one place. It was a good thing that my reservations had been made almost six months in advance.

Some of the pre-Lenten excitement rubbed off on me. I pulled out my cell phone to call home.

"Mom, I'm here, safe in one piece. As soon as I check in, I'll give you the phone and room number."

When it was my turn to check in, I gave the reservations clerk my name. She tapped the keyboard and frowned.

"I'm sorry, but there is no reservation here for you. Maybe your name is misspelled in the computer. Let's try it, again."

We did, but there was no luck. "But I made these reservations six months ago!"

When she had done all she could, I was afraid and frustrated. Where else could I get a reservation on the weekend of Mardi Gras? It looked like everybody in the country had converged on this city, and they had gotten here ahead of me Or could I even get a flight back home at this time of day?

"Excuse me, Miss. Maybe I can help you. Let me just speak to the desk clerk."

I turned to see a tanned, slender man standing behind me. He was well built and tanned, as if he had just come from long vacation in the sun. The clothes he wore were casual and fit him well.

He stepped ahead of me and spoke in a soft voice to the clerk. When he finished, she looked over at me and smiled. I let go of the breath I had been holding, and gave my mind a rest from the scrambled thoughts about what in the world I would do.

When he bowed slightly, his eyes twinkled.

"I think we have it taken care of, now. You can pick up your room keys, and stop holding your breath."

I laughed as much from relief as from his witty remark.

"Thank you so very much. I don't know what I would have done. Probably had to sleep on the street."

"Oh believe me, if you tried to sleep, you wouldn't get a wink with all the fun being had out there." He nodded in the direction of the street. "But I'll let you get settled in. Enjoy your stay and Mardi Gras."

When the bellman deposited me in my room, it was nothing like I expected. Nor what I paid for. This was obviously a luxury suite that I couldn't have afforded—even if I ate pork and beans all year. Better not get too comfortable, my inner voice warned. I touched the number that connected me to the front desk.

"Uh, this is Lauren Holder. I think I have the wrong room. This couldn't be the one I paid for."

Her laughter did nothing to calm my fears that just as soon as I settled in, I'd be out on the street again for the inability to pay my bill.

"Mr. Crane took care of it. Don't worry; you'll only be charged the regular rate."

"Who is Mr. Crane?"

All I needed was some guy trying to set me up for a little more fun than I intended.

"Mr. Crane is the general manager of the company that owns this hotel. I guess you can say he has the run of the place," she chuckled.

I sat back down on the bed. On the one hand, I couldn't get back home if I tried—at least tonight. And where would I go? But if this man is the general manager, he probably wouldn't be trying anything funny—especially with a complete stranger who wasn't looking her most glamorous.

I decided to stop looking for trouble and instead, look for something to eat. The information booklet on the desk listed the hotel restaurants and their menus. Since New Orleans was famed for its food, it looked like I was in for a treat. The hostess seated me at a table near the window, where I could see a lot of the action out on the street. The city looked like something from another world with the two-story buildings and their lacy wrought iron railings. I saw people on the second story calling down and throwing beads to the pedestrians below. And talk about flashing—I saw more boobs than a breast surgeon that night. When one poor soul attempted to climb up the post, he couldn't hold on and slid down as if he were holding onto a greased pig. I later found out that the pole had been greased, to keep that very thing from happening.

When my gumbo came, I was in heaven. For that, I didn't mind dining alone. All my attention was paid to the delicious meal in front of me, until I looked up to see Thomas Crane standing next to me. He had changed into dark brown slacks with a knife-sharp crease and an oyster-colored shirt and looked like money, money, money.

"Thank you so much!" I exclaimed. "The suite is beautiful and a whole lot more than I expected. I really do appreciate it. You saved my life."

"You're very welcome. Even though I joked about it, being stranded without a hotel in New Orleans—especially during Mardi Gras, is no fun. And it was obviously a mistake on our part, so there was no question that we make it up to you. I'm glad to be of assistance."

When he left, I wondered how old he was. There was no gray in his hair, and he had a young man's face, but he carried himself with an assurance that gave him an air of maturity. Maybe it was the combination of his job and the money he obviously had. Later on, when I slid between those cool, luxurious sheets, I slept like a newborn baby. The next morning was my day to explore.

Someone told me I couldn't be in New Orleans and not eat beignets at Café Du Monde. I stood in the lobby, consulting my flyer for directions when Thomas Crane strode toward me.

"Need some help?"

"Knowing the way I follow directions, I probably do. Instead of Café du Monde, I'd probably end up on the airport runway."

Crane threw back his head and laughed.

"I love your sense of humor. Would you allow me to escort you to the café, and then stay with you just in case you can't find your way back?"

Merriment shone in his eyes. Why not? I had a feeling that as much as I intended to enjoy myself, it would even better with another person—especially a person like him. He looked like class and money, but he still had that man thing going on—a thing I hadn't paid attention to in a long while.

After my first bite of the beignet, I closed my eyes as if in prayer.

"They're delicious, aren't they?" Thomas clearly enjoyed watching me eat.

I couldn't speak; I just nodded my head and chewed.

"I hope I can find a recipe for these things, because I'll never be able to live without them."

Instead of delivering me back to the hotel, Thomas ended up taking me on a walking tour of the French Quarter.

"Don't you have to get back to work?" I asked over a lunch of fried oyster po' boys.

"Ah, when you're kind of the boss, you set your own hours. "Besides", he laughed. "I am at work. I'm promoting New Orleans tourism to a guest of my hotel."

When it was time to go back to the hotel, all of a sudden, I didn't want my tour guide to leave me. He was easy to talk to, and extremely knowledgeable about the culture and customs of the Big Easy. When I wanted to see the Garden District, or Anne Rice's house, he produced a car and whisked me around for a more personal tour than I would have gotten, otherwise. And not only was he easy to talk to, he was very easy on the eyes. I liked the way I felt in his presence. However, he was a busy man, and had done more for a stranded tourist than could be expected. I chalked it up to an unexpected treat and vowed to spend the rest of my trip on my own.

That evening, when my room phone rang, I thought it might be the desk clerk telling me that my Cinderella ride was over, and it was time to wash dishes or get out.

"Hello, Lauren. Are you worn out from today, or are you ready for some real New Orleans fun? Your tour guide is ready and waiting."

I couldn't believe it! Maybe that New Orleans voodoo magic was working. Indeed, I was ready for some New Orleans, Thomas Crane-style fun!

That night, the street was dense with people. It was nearly impossible to move without bumping into someone. That's when Thomas took my hand, to make sure we didn't get separated. Even when the crowed thinned, his hand remained folded around mine.

"I know it's kind of touristy, but when you get back home, you can tell your family that you sampled one of the famous hurricanes at Pat O'Brien's. I guess because Thomas knew someone, we managed to snag a table. Everybody in the city must be crammed into the three bars and patio of that place. After a few sips of the hurricane, I felt like I was in a pleasant rippling breeze.

"What brought you to New Orleans at this time of year, alone?" Thomas asked.

The drink loosened my tongue, and I told him the story of my broken engagement. I told him that instead of having a sad memory of what would have been, I wanted to make new memories of my own.

Instead of the amused expression I was used to, he gave me one I couldn't read.

"Please forgive me for speaking plainly, but it was the best thing that could have happened to you."

"It's okay," I replied. "I kind of came to that conclusion somewhere along the line."

"A woman like you have would have withered. You would have spent all your time trying to make it work, or trying to figure out why it wasn't working—instead of being your lovely, spirited self."

I didn't have a quick, flippant answer for that one, even with the aid of the potent drink. "Thank you for saying that to me. For paying enough attention. And for helping me have a much better time than I would have on my own."

It was the right time and place for Thomas to cover my hand with his. When we left Pat O'Brien's, it was more than right for him to keep hold of me—even when there was more than enough room on the sidewalk for us to maneuver. At the door to my room, Thomas first drew my hand to his lips, before placing a kiss on my forehead.

"Tomorrow?" he whispered.

"Of course," I smiled back.

It was Sunday, and if it was possible, there was even more of an air of high excitement. People strolled the streets with open containers of liquor—something that would have gotten them arrested almost anywhere else in the country. I had seen a bit of the Mardi Gras Indians, resplendent in their feathered costumes. It was like nothing I had ever seen in the world, and if I hadn't been with Thomas, I would have never known about that part of New Orleans culture. I was giddy when we danced the second line. If I had been home, I would have been moping, but here, I got a new lease on life that would last me long after I returned to my little cottage.

Thomas and I walked back to the hotel. I was tired, sticky, and wanted a shower. One thing I didn't want to do was to miss any more of the unique flavor of anything that remotely had to do with Mardi and New Orleans.

"If you like, I'll pick you up for dinner. I know you have a couple more days here, and I'd like to spend them with you, as much as I can. You're quite a woman."

When Thomas left me at my door, if someone had screwed a light into my head, it would have lit up the entire state of Louisiana.

Dinner was nothing like I expected—nothing like the funky, fun dinners we'd shared. He took me to a private alcove off the main dining area. Everything was done in white: glittering white tapers, creamy white tablecloth, and a breathtaking arrangement of white roses. Even the chairs had been covered from top to bottom in sheer white cotton and tied at the back with a huge bow.

"Oh, my goodness! I stared at the luxurious table setting and back at Thomas. "This is so very wonderful and beautiful. How did this happen?"

He gave me a half smile. "Remember, I'm kind of in charge, so I get to do a few things out of the ordinary. And for you, for Valentine's Day, I wanted this.

I clapped my hand over my mouth.

"Valentine's Day!"

I hadn't even remembered."

"Well then, I've done my job, because not one thought of lost love entered your mind."

He stood behind me and pulled out my chair. We had one server at our disposal to serve our wine, appetizers, main course, and dessert. He stood discreetly to the side, far enough away from our conversation, but close enough to bring whatever we wanted or needed.

Thomas steepled his hands in front of his face.

"I know you were curious, but too gracious to ask, about me. So let me tell you. As you know, I'm general manager of the group that owns this chain. I started young, right out of college with this company, and worked my way up. Actually, the job was therapy for me."

"Therapy?" How so?"

"When I was in my last year of college, I met the woman whom I considered the love of my life. I pursued her, and we got married. Three years into it, she lost interest in marriage. She told me that she had always wanted to be an artist, but that the life of a wife and mother would be too restrictive, too confining for too long."

"So why did she marry you?"

"Because we had gone too far in the preparations to back out. She wanted to save face. See why I told you that your broken engagement was the best thing that could have happened?"

It was the best thing that could have happened in so many ways. Just like Craig, I hadn't been away from my cocoon to experience any of the world outside what was familiar to me. Now, not only had I left my comfort zone, but I met a successful, accomplished man who was still down to earth enough to appreciate me as I was. That dinner drew us closer, and even though I would be going back home, I didn't believe Thomas would be out of my life for good.

"Our evening isn't finished, yet," Thomas told me as gathered the white flowers for me to carry. "It's out front."

When we got to the lobby, I nearly cried out. A horse and carriage waited outside, with a bouquet of roses on the passenger's seat. When I stepped up, I felt like Cinderella. Thomas put his arm around me, and I laid my head on his shoulder while we rode around the beautiful, quiet areas of the city—far away from the Sunday night revelers.

When it was time to go, my feelings were bittersweet. I had to go home, but I didn't want this wonderful time to end. Then, I realized that leaving as it was right now would preserve it forever in my mind.

57

Thomas and I kissed at the airport, and I hoped he wouldn't forget me as soon as my plane took off.

He did not. Over the months that followed, we saw each other often. He sent for me for long weekends and whenever he was anywhere near my part of the country, I saw him. "We're on to something, don't you think," he teased. "Want to make something of it?"

"Yes, I do," I whispered, snuggling up to him on my porch swing.

The End

I DELIVERED DEATH FOR
VALENTINE'S DAY
I Don't Know Why He Hired Me

Dressed in my red lace teddy, I opened the bathroom door. I planted a hand on my hip and looked at my husband, willing him to notice my seductive Valentine's Day ensemble.

"Stephanie? Have you seen my new shirt?"

"I ironed it last night. It's hanging in the laundry room. But, why don't you wear the red one, since it's—"

"Thanks, honey." Ian's gaze never dropped below my face. "I'm out the door—as soon as I get my shirt on. See you this evening." He leaned forward and pecked my cheek, smelling of cologne and toothpaste.

The moment the door was shut, I threw my brush against it in a fit of frustration. He hadn't noticed! Which meant that it was likely that he wouldn't remember to buy me flowers or candy—again.

Four years of marriage and only one year of flowers and candy on Valentine's Day. What had happened to the romance? When I had met Ian, I'd thought that he was the most romantic man in the world.

It was one of the reasons why I'd married him!

Little had I known that morning that that Valentine's Day would eventually turn out to be one I would never forget. . . .

"Um, honey?" Ian asked through the door.

His voice had startled me because I'd thought that he'd gone.

"Yes?" My heart filled with hope. I thought that maybe he was going to wish me a happy Valentine's Day, and tell me that we would be going out later that evening.

"I'm going to be late tonight. I've got an office meeting that I can't miss," he told me.

Well, that's just great, I thought, wiping my streaming eyes. I sniffled, feeling sorry for myself. What's happened to our marriage? To the romance?

When I was sure that he was gone, I left the bathroom and finished dressing. I worked at a gourmet candy shop, and I knew that it was going to be a busy day. There'd be lots of women whose men would be buying them some delicious candy, or an adorable stuffed animal.

At least, it'll be a great day for some lucky girls. Not me, though, I thought.

Although I wasn't in the mood, I picked out a red suit that I'd bought the year before to go with the red teddy. I rummaged in my jewelry box and found my Cupid earrings. After I'd grabbed my red purse, I was ready to go.

I was determined not to spread my gloom, so I pasted a false smile on my face on the way to work. Daphne, my boss, had told me that I'd be working the counter that day, while she and the other members of the staff worked in the back, filling special mail orders.

I had counter duty along with Lynnette and Misty—college girls who worked mostly during the holidays.

The moment I put away my purse and approached the counter, Lynnette thrust her hand beneath my nose. She had a huge grin on her face, and her eyes were literally sparkling.

"Look what I found on my pillow this morning!" she exclaimed, turning her hand so that the overhead light caught the huge diamond ring on her finger. "Right next to a perfect rose. Isn't Barry just wonderful?"

Gamely, I held my brittle smile as I admired her ring. It really was lovely.

"Yes, he must be. Congratulations," I murmured.

"Thanks, Stephanie. I'm sure it's nothing new to you, though, huh? That hunk of man you're married to probably gives you gifts on a regular basis."

Shame on me for lying, but for the life of me, I couldn't help it. Pride goeth before a fall, as they always said.

"Yes, Ian does things like that all the time." I was grateful that Daphne wasn't around to hear that big whopper! She was my friend, and she knew just how disgusted I was with Ian those days.

Proud of myself for not spoiling their pleasure just because I had none, I turned from the bubbling Lynnette and glanced at a glowing Misty.

My heart sank at the gleam in her eye. I gave an inward sigh and braced myself for another cup of salt in the wound.

"Good morning, Stephanie," she chirped.

"Good morning, Misty," I responded brightly. And then, despite my good intentions, I went on. "And what did you wake up to this morning? An enormous bouquet of flowers? A diamond necklace? A fur coat?"

Misty, unaware of my sarcasm, laughed. "Nothing that great, I'm afraid. Alec's treating me to a night on the town. We're going out to dinner and then, we're going dancing."

Alec was Misty's fiancé. They'd been going together for three years.

Okay, I told myself. A night on the town. It isn't a huge, sparkling diamond. I can handle that.

"And, he gave me this!" Misty suddenly shrieked, scaring the life out of me as she swung her hand in front of my face.

It was a ring—a square-cut emerald ring, surrounded by sparkling diamonds.

I was saved from making a blubbering fool of myself as the bells chimed, signaling a customer. Since Misty and Lynnette immediately became engrossed in gushing over one another's rings, I waited on the customer.

"Can I help you?" I asked politely, thinking that the guy certainly was handsome. Young, but handsome. I figured that he was twenty—possibly twenty-one. He reminded me of a movie star.

"I'm sure you can," he drawled, flashing me a heart-stopping smile.

My own smile became genuine. "Let me guess: You want to send your sweetheart a box of candy."

He nodded, still smiling in a way that made me, a happily—at least most of the time—married woman, breathless.

I'm still young, I reminded myself. And human. Besides, there's nothing wrong with a little drooling. It's Ian's fault, anyway, for making me feel unloved.

"Actually, I have three sweethearts," he said.

I was speechless for a second. Three? So, he wasn't so great. He was a two-timing—make that three-timing—man. And it was, of course, none of my business.

He must have read the disapproval in my eyes, though, because he laughed.

"I've been gone for a few years, and I just want to put out some feelers—see who's still available in the dating game," he explained.

"Oh." There was no sense in trying to deny what I was thinking, I supposed, since it was apparently written all over my face. With an inward, wistful sigh, I decided to get back to business. "What would you like to order?"

"What have you got?" he asked.

Dutifully, I handed him a brochure that Daphne had put together for Valentine's Day, hoping that customers would stick to the things that she had ready, or that she could get ready in no time flat.

After a brief inspection of the brochure, he pointed to our most popular item—a beautifully decorated box filled with heart-shaped chocolates.

"Good choice," I told him, flashing him a professional smile. I could do it, I decided. I could be happy for everyone else who was having a wonderful Valentine's Day.

Okay, so I did envy Lynnette and Misty—and the three lucky ladies who were the hunky man's targets.

"I'll need three of those." He reached into his pocket and brought out a piece of paper. "Here are the names and the addresses."

"And your name?" I figured that it would be a wonderful name, something strong and elegant. . . .

"No name." His smile was mysterious. "I want them to think and wonder first, before I let them know who sent them."

Since I couldn't insist on a name, I had no choice but to abide by his wishes.

"Any particular time?" I asked.

"Oh, yes. Time is very important. I want them delivered exactly at the times I've specified by each name, starting with the girl at the top of the list." He leaned forward so suddenly that I jerked back. "The timing has to be precise—do you understand?"

A strange shiver tiptoed down my spine as I gazed into his bright eyes. There was something odd about those eyes, I decided. They looked almost fanatical. With an inward, scornful laugh at myself, I shrugged it off. Silly me. I was just a poor, neglected housewife looking for excitement in the eyes of a stranger.

"We'll deliver them exactly as you say," I told him, tallying up the bill. "Would you like to enclose a card with them?" His request meant that the last valentine would have to be delivered at seven o'clock, but since I had nothing planned, I didn't mention that we closed at five. I figured I could make the delivery on the way home.

"Yes. I want it to say, 'Your secret admirer,'" he instructed.

How original, I thought. I kept my opinions to myself, of course, as I scribbled his request on a sheet of paper.

Just a single red rose, I thought as I took the man's money and counted out his change. If Ian would give me just a single rose, I would be delirious. He wouldn't have had to go all out like that guy was doing—I wasn't that hard to please. In fact, a simple "Happy Valentine's Day" and a good, long, passionate kiss would probably have appeased me.

Pitiful, but true.

"Remember," the man said, "the timing has to be precise."

"Gotcha." I watched him as he left. The moment the door closed behind him, I mumbled, "Cute, but creepy."

Misty came to stand beside me, and we both watched through the window as the stranger got into his car and drove away.

"Ooh, sexy," she purred.

"He's having a Valentine's Day special sent to three different women," I said, almost gleefully. I instantly felt ashamed. Darn Ian— he was turning me into a shrew!

But to my secret, shameful disappointment, Misty wasn't put off by my revelation.

"I'm not surprised. He looks as if it would take more than one woman to satisfy him," she commented.

62

I wondered snidely if Misty would feel that way if it were her boyfriend who was sending the gifts to different women.

"So," Lynnette said, joining us at the counter, "who's going to do the delivering today? Want to draw straws?"

"I will," I said impulsively. "I want to make the deliveries." I thought that maybe if I kept busy, I wouldn't think so much about Ian and his insensitivity.

"Fine with me," Misty said, sounding relieved.

"Me, too," Lynette echoed.

I decided to call the mystery man "Casanova." His first delivery was scheduled for one o'clock, so I left shortly after he did. On the way, I couldn't help wondering if the women would be home, and if they were, how he'd known that they would be.

But, it was none of my business. My business was to deliver candy for Valentine's Day—a holiday my husband apparently thought was frivolous and not worth remembering. Apparently, I wasn't worth thinking about, either.

I gave myself a stern lecture as I got out of the car and retrieved the first beautifully wrapped box from the back. I was just doing my job. I would be enthusiastic and upbeat, and I would not, I repeated to myself, be a stick in the mud. The recipients would never know how much I envied them.

The first woman answered the door of her apartment a little impatiently, as if she'd already been disturbed by someone.

"Yes?" she snapped.

I glanced at the name on the card. "Donna Jorgenson?" I asked.

"That's me," she replied hesitantly.

By that time, the woman had noticed the box in my arms.

"Is that for me?" she breathed, her eyes glittering with excitement.

"Yes, it is." I swallowed a lump of envy and handed the box to her. "The chocolates are exquisite," I told her.

She giggled, still looking wondrous. "Who sent this?" she asked.

"He didn't leave a name," I answered.

"Oh, please! You've got to tell me! Chocolates are my favorite."

"I really don't know. He didn't leave a name," I repeated.

Ms. Jorgenson apparently didn't believe me. "Was it Norman?"

"I don't know," I said patiently, thinking to myself that the guy hadn't looked like a Norman.

"Steven?" she persisted.

"Like I said, he didn't leave a name." I decided that the woman was either deaf, or just plain dumb.

"You're lying," she told me suddenly.

Her sudden accusation had left me speechless. When I'd finally found my tongue, I knew that my face was red.

"Look, Ms. Jorgenson. I've already explained that he didn't leave a name, which is the truth. If he had left a name and requested anonymity, then I still wouldn't be able to tell you. But, I can assure you that he did not leave a name."

"Oh." A puzzled frown marred her pretty face. "Well, can you describe him?" Her frown melted into a dreamy expression. "Was he a hunk? Tall? Handsome? Did he look rich?"

Deciding that there wasn't any harm in telling her what I could, I did. I gave her a description of the gorgeous guy who'd sent the gift.

Ms. Jorgenson laughed. "That describes about half of the men that I've dated!"

Well, lucky you, I thought, swallowing my catty remark. "Well, enjoy your candy, and Happy Valentine's Day," I told her.

"Yeah, thanks," she said as she shut the door in my face.

I made a few more deliveries, then returned to the shop. I helped at the counter for an hour or so, then picked up my second of Casanova's orders.

Ms. Stringfield, Casanova's second choice, answered the door dressed in an oversized T-shirt, jeans, and no makeup. Still, even without the makeup, I thought that she was pretty—and lucky.

"I have a delivery for you," I began, handing her the box. I turned, hoping to get away before the questions started.

I didn't make it, though.

"Wait! You can't just leave me hanging like this! Who are they from?" she asked eagerly.

Slowly, I turned. I sighed, then gave a fatalistic shrug. "I don't know. He didn't leave his name."

"Oh." She looked disappointed.

I started to leave again, mumbling a prayer beneath my breath.

"What did he look like?" she called after me.

Retracing my steps, I came back to the door, repeating my earlier description almost verbatim.

"He sounds good," Ms. Stringfield said, licking her lips as if she could already taste him. "Are you certain that he didn't leave his name?"

"I'm certain," I assured her, and turned to walk away again.

"Wait!" she pleaded.

Once again, I stopped and turned to face her.

Ms. Stringfield disappeared from the doorway, then returned a few seconds later. She handed me a twenty-dollar bill. "Now, will you tell me who he is?" she asked coyly.

Calmly, I handed her back the twenty. "Honestly, he didn't leave his name," I insisted, repeating each word slowly.

Finally, it seemed as though she'd actually gotten the message. "This will drive me insane," she announced.

I sympathized. Getting an anonymous Valentine's Day gift would have driven me insane, too.

Insanely happy, maybe.

Before I made my third and final delivery, I told Daphne—who looked ready to drop from exhaustion—that I would lock up if she wanted to go on home. I didn't add that I had nothing planned for the evening, although I could have used a good ear and some advice about Ian.

With a grateful smile, she thanked me and went home to her husband and three children, whom, she said, had made her a special Valentine's Day dinner.

My false spirits lagged dangerously on hearing that, but I managed to hide them from my boss. She left without knowing just how low her employee and friend had sunk.

I tidied up before gathering my final delivery, pocketing the keys that Daphne had entrusted to me. On the way, I found myself hoping that the one last, luscious, lucky woman wouldn't be home. I just wasn't up to another ecstatic female when the only thing waiting for me at home was a load of laundry and a few dirty dishes in the sink.

As rotten luck would have it, Ms. Tiffany Seymour was home, and very eager to get a Valentine's Day gift from a secret admirer.

She was also—surprise, surprise—another gorgeous woman.

"Oh, my goodness!" She literally danced in place when she saw the beautifully wrapped box. "Oh, wow! Who was it? What did he look like? Oh, please let it have been Ryan!"

I didn't know anyone named Ryan. Of course, her secret admirer could have been named Ryan, for all that I knew. "He was really good looking," I said, warming to my now-familiar recital. I proceeded to give a thorough description of her secret admirer.

Ms. Seymour's face fell. "Oh," she said sadly. "Ryan doesn't look anything like that. Are you sure?"

It was on the tip of my sharp tongue to tell her that I wasn't likely to forget the man's incredible good looks, but I held myself back. It wasn't their fault, I reminded myself, that Ian was an insensitive jerk—or that they were lucky, loved, and admired.

"Yes, I'm positive," I said instead. "Maybe he's an old boyfriend?" I hadn't given that much of a hint to the other three, but I figured that it wouldn't hurt.

Ms. Seymour laughed. "Oh, that's funny! Do you have any idea of how many handsome men I've dated?"

I didn't, and neither did I care to speculate. I was a bit disgusted that she would brag. "I'm sorry. Maybe you'll figure it out," I said coldly.

On the way home—to my empty house—I stopped to get a bottle

of wine and a couple of lobsters. I decided that I would fix a late meal and light candles, hoping to put Ian in the mood—and remind him of the holiday.

While putting my groceries in the backseat, I saw the card, realizing that I must have dropped it when I'd been retrieving the box of candy.

"Shoot," I mumbled, undecided about what to do. The card should have been delivered with the candy, and if I didn't return and give it to Ms. Seymour, she might find out and complain.

And, I didn't want to embarrass Daphne.

With a few muffled curses, I got in my car and turned around, heading back to Ms. Seymour's apartment. When I got there, I rushed inside and up the stairs, deciding that it would be quicker than waiting for the elevator.

I was panting by the time I reached her apartment door. With the card in my hand, I reached out and pressed my thumb against the buzzer.

Almost immediately, I heard a scream from inside.

It wasn't just a tiny scream. It wasn't just Ms. Seymour screaming for me to wait.

It was a piercing, terrified scream that sent goose bumps racing across my skin. It was a cry for help—for mercy.

The scream was abruptly muffled. Then, I heard footsteps inside the apartment, coming to the door.

Without another thought as to why I was running, I turned and stumbled to the stairs. I nearly fell in my haste—my heart was racing as I ran to the car.

At any moment, I expected a hand to reach out and grasp my shoulder, or a voice to yell out for me to stop. As if I'd ever even consider doing such a thing!

I fumbled for my keys, desperate to put distance between myself and those ominous footsteps. When I finally got the car started, I squealed out of the parking lot. The shop was closer than home, I figured, so I put the pedal to the metal and headed that way. I decided that I would go there and call the police.

Maybe I was being foolish, and maybe I wasn't. But it didn't hurt to be safe, I told myself as I braked sharply into front of the candy shop.

When I stepped out of the car, I realized that I didn't have the card with me. I must have dropped it in the hall.

The realization—and the possible implications—turned my feet into wings. I unlocked the door to the shop and rushed inside, turning to lock the door. My breath came in sharp, painful bursts. My heart threatened to burst right out of my chest. My legs felt like cooked noodles, and would hardly support me as I staggered to the counter.

Whom should I call? My first instinct was to call Ian, but I reluctantly discarded that idea. He probably wasn't home, and if he wasn't, then I would have wasted time.

If whoever had been in that apartment had found the card in the hall, then he would have known that I had heard the scream. He might come after me. In fact, I made myself admit, chances were that it was Casanova who would come after me.

I reached for the phone and began to dial.

Before I could finish, I found myself hanging up. Doubts had suddenly assailed me. What if the scream I'd heard hadn't been one of terror? What if Ms. Seymour had been participating in a little rough-and-tumble sex? What if my overactive, bored imagination had just imagined her scream as one of terror, and it had, in fact, had nothing to do with Casanova?

And, what if I sent the police over there and they came back laughing at me?

With that thought in mind, I searched in my coat pocket for the list of names and addresses of the people that I had delivered packages to earlier that day. My hands shook as I dialed information and asked for Donna Jorgenson's number. She was the first on the list. The operator thanked me, then gave me the number.

I dialed the number, and my hands were clenched as I waited for someone to answer. The phone rang a few times before someone picked up.

"Jorgenson residence," a cryptic male voice answered.

My voice shook. "Could I speak to Donna, please?" I asked.

"May I ask who's calling?" the man demanded sharply.

I swallowed hard. "Is she there?" I persisted.

"Are you a relative?" he asked.

A wave of chilling premonition swept over me. "No. I—I delivered a box of candy to her earlier—"

"What's your name, ma'am?" he persisted.

I quickly hung up. I don't know why—I just did. I supposed that I was just too scared to think straight.

Something bad had happened to Donna Jorgenson, I was certain.

And, something bad was happening to Ms. Seymour, as well. Feeling on the verge of total hysteria, I picked up the phone once again and dialed 911. In a shaky voice, I told the dispatcher about my suspicions.

"You've got to get someone over there right now! I think she's being murdered!" I cried hysterically.

If I was wrong, I could live with that. But, if I wasn't, and I did nothing, then I knew that I could not live with the guilt.

"Ma'am, can I get your name and number?" the dispatcher asked.

I quickly gave her the information, then hung up, biting my nails as I decided what to do next. I should go home, I decided. Once Ian arrived, I would have him to lean on. He would know what to do.

As I struggled into my coat again, I heard a noise at the door.

I froze, turning slowly.

It was Casanova, and he stared at me through the glass with a purpose in his eyes that I didn't care to define. His previously neat hair was unruly, and the freshly pressed suit that he'd worn earlier was a wrinkled mess. He looked as though he'd been in a fight with someone, and it didn't take much for me to figure out who that someone had been.

Donna Jorgenson.

With a panicked shriek, I grabbed the phone. It slipped from my fumbling fingers and crashed to the floor.

I heard breaking glass, and I looked up just in time to see Casanova reach his hand inside the broken window and unlock the door. He was still watching me with deadly intent.

My heart felt as though it had stuttered to a stop. Frantically, I searched for a place to run, knowing that I had no time to call the police.

My gaze landed on Daphne's office door. I tried desperately to remember if she had a lock on the door, then decided that it didn't matter. I figured that I could push the desk against the door, then use her phone to call the police.

The front door crashed open, slamming against the wall and spilling the rest of the glass onto the floor.

Oh, no! I thought wildly. This can't be happening to me! I lunged for the office, literally fell inside, then slammed the door closed. I stood there for a second, panting—scared out of my wits.

Then, I moved like lightning. I grabbed the edge of the desk and shoved with all my might, inching the heavy piece of furniture toward the door.

At any moment, I expected Casanova to come crashing through, foiling my plans, and grabbing me before I'd had a chance to barricade myself in the office.

Just as the desk connected with the door, Casanova slammed into it. For one insane moment, I nearly laughed at his failure. Then, I remembered what I should have been doing.

I grabbed for the phone and began to jab at the numbers. A woman answered the 911 call, but before I could tell her my name and what was happening, the phone went dead. Staring at the dead phone in shock, I let it slip from my numb fingers. It was no good to me anymore.

I was trapped—and on the other side of the door, a killer waited for me. Slowly, I slid to the floor, my eyes glued to the barricaded door. He'd have to be really strong to get in, I reminded my terror-stricken mind.

Okay, so he had looked strong, but not that strong. Not superhero strong.

Suddenly, Casanova lunged against the door, startling a shriek out of me. The desk moved an inch.

It was an inch too far, in my opinion. I scrambled along the floor until I was between the desk and the wall. Bracing my feet against the desk leg, I then braced my back against the wall, adding to the weight of the barricade.

The next time he lunged, the vibration traveled through the desk, along my legs, and jarred my teeth.

There was no doubt that he meant business—that he was determined not to leave a witness to his crimes. And, I was definitely a witness. In fact, I had unwittingly helped him. I had paved the way, gushing over his perfect manners, his good looks, his beautiful eyes, and his sexy smile.

I had teased his victims to the point where they had probably dragged him eagerly into their homes. Oh, what in the world had I done?

I shrieked again as something hard and heavy hit the door. I heard a grunt, then muffled cursing. It sounded as if Casanova were scuffling with someone. I dared to hope that that someone had noticed the shattered glass and had stopped to investigate.

But, what if Casanova killed them, too? What would happen then? Who would rescue me?

I shoved my fist into my mouth to still my terrified moans so that I could listen. There was more scuffling, more cursing, and the distinct sound of fists colliding with flesh.

Yes! I thought, my hopes rising. Casanova is fighting with someone!

On the verge of shouting for help, I quickly checked myself. I didn't want to distract my savior, whoever it was. So I sat there in silence, scared to death, urging my unknown rescuer on.

The fight seemed to go on forever. Finally, there was one last thump against the door, then only silence from the other side.

I counted to a hundred, then slowly got to my feet. Crawling across the desk, I put my ear to the door. I could hear someone breathing. When I heard a voice, I nearly swallowed my tongue in fear.

"Stephanie? Are you in there? Are you okay?"

It was Ian! Shaking, sobbing, and laughing at the same time, I scrambled from the desk and tugged it away from the door. I broke a few nails in the process, but I didn't care.

I hesitated only an instant before I opened the door.

Ian stood there, looking wild-eyed and breathing as if he'd just run a marathon. A stream of blood ran down his chin from his bruised nose. My stunned gaze dripped to his bleeding, swollen knuckles.

It took me a few moments to realize that he wore a tuxedo—or, what was left of it. The jacket was missing, and his white, ruffled, shirt was open from his neck to his waist, revealing a trail of bloody scratches on his chest.

We stared at each other for a long moment. Ian was the first to move. He glanced around him on the floor as if searching for something. Finally, he spotted it. I watched, unable to move, as he retrieved the bouquet and came back to where I stood, hugging the doorway as if my life depended on it.

Well, my legs did depend on it.

He handed me the bedraggled bunch of tulips with a sheepish smile that melted my heart on the spot.

"I had planned to take you out to a fancy restaurant, but I guess maybe we should go home and change first."

Tulips. Not your typical roses, but tulips—my favorite. Ian had not only remembered that they were my favorite flowers, but he had planned to take me out to dinner. And, he had saved my life.

Now that, I thought a bit smugly, tops a diamond ring.

My hand shook badly as I took the tulips from his bleeding hand. I dropped the flowers on the floor and took his hand instead, tenderly kissing each bruised knuckle. Tears welled in my eyes and spilled over my cheeks.

"Hey, you," Ian said softly, pulling me to him and enfolding me in the warm security of his arms. He gestured with a nod to the unconscious guy on the floor. "Did you annoy this guy or something?"

I pressed my cheek against his pounding heart. "Something like that," I murmured. "I love you."

"I love you, too." His voice sounded suddenly shaky and thick. "When I pulled in and saw the shattered glass, I nearly went berserk, thinking that something had happened to you."

"Something nearly did," I told him, shuddering at the memory. My voice dropped to a whisper. "I think I delivered valentines for a killer, Ian. I think I helped him—"

"Hush now, sweetie." Ian swept a comforting hand over my hair. "You couldn't have known, honey. You couldn't have known." He released one arm and began digging into his jacket pocket. When he held up his cell phone, he flashed me a sheepish smile. "I was going to turn it off when we got to the restaurant—I swear."

I held onto him as he called the police. Then, together, we tied Casanova's hands and feet with shiny red ribbon, the same ribbon that

70

Daphne had used to decorate the boxes of candy that he'd bought for his victims. The irony didn't escape me.

Later, I learned that in interrupting Casanova during his attack on Ms. Seymour, I had saved her life. Yet, I didn't know if I could ever quite banish the feelings of guilt that I experienced each time I thought about that day.I had inadvertently helped Casanova gain admission into the homes of the women that he'd killed.

Some people have called me a heroine. I just call myself lucky.

And, as for Ian? Well, I call him my knight in shining armor.

The End

THIS CAN'T BE LOVE...
Especially When You Pay For It!

The auctioneer's voice bellowed above the din of the crowd. "Sold!" His gavel came down like a shot being fired, ending the bidding, and sealing my fate. I'd been sold like common cattle to a man I'd met only hours before.

I blinked back tears of shame and humiliation, wishing I could hide my face from the sea of onlookers. It was the most embarrassing moment of my life, and I'd brought the entire thing on myself.

It all started a week before Valentine's Day. You have to understand that February 14th had never been my favorite day of the year. It always seemed like everyone else had someone special, while I'd be left sitting at home with a TV dinner and reruns of old sitcoms. But not this year. Everything was about to change.

I'd zipped myself into my work uniform and walked out into the cool evening air. Even in south Texas, February could get pretty chilly, and I was glad to have a warm sweater over my shoulders.

It was almost dark, and as I slid into the driver's seat of my used compact car, I glanced back at the white wood frame duplex where I'd lived alone for the past few years. Lately, it felt more and more like a prison--a neat, pretty prison, with potted plants on the front porch and cozy peach curtains in the window. It was confining and lonely.

I worked nights waiting tables at Worthington's Restaurant. I worked extra shifts whenever I could for spare cash. Worthington's was a nice place—a little pricey for me—but the tips were good. Still, the hours were long, leaving me exhausted. I usually came home, pried my comfortable soft-soled shoes from my aching feet, and fell asleep on the couch with the TV going in the background. Other than work, I had no life to speak of—unless you counted weekly visits to my mom in the next town.

I was almost always alone.

Driving to the restaurant that February night, I passed florists and gift shops with Valentine displays in the windows. Candy and flowers, teddy bears and cards, and beautiful pink and red tokens of love for the person you couldn't live without.

That was something I'd never experienced. I've always been on the heavy side, and it kept guys from looking twice at me. I was twenty-eight years old, and I had never had a boyfriend.

A red light halted my progress. I came to a stop, glancing at a lingerie display in a store window on the corner. My eyes shot down to my neatly pressed black-and-white uniform and my sensible shoes.

I never wore anything remotely sexy. I kept my naturally blond hair nicely styled, but I never bothered with much makeup. And I was too self-conscious, too embarrassed by my extra curves, to wear anything that wasn't at least one size too large. I let out a sigh, and I put my foot on the accelerator when the light changed.

That's when I noticed it. The car bucked and halted in an all too familiar way.

"Not this again," I said to myself, stepping on the accelerator. The car lurched forward with an angry gurgle and refused to move any further.

It had done this before, and I had the repair bills to prove it.

Holding my breath, I said a quick prayer for the car to get me to and from work safely. Someone must've been listening, because I pulled into the parking lot at Worthington's without a hitch. With a whispered thanks to God, I got out of the car and went inside to start my shift.

"It's the housing on your carburetor cables," Greg, one of the waiters said, as he shook his head, arranging salads on a tray. "That could run into a lot of money."

I took a long sip of my diet soda and tried not to panic. "Are you sure? Couldn't it be something . . . less expensive? I had to live on canned soup for a month to pay for getting those things fixed last time." Greg knew a lot about cars, and I usually trusted him to help me keep mine up and running. But just this once, I hoped he'd be wrong.

He shrugged. "I suppose it could be something else. But it sounds exactly like what happened to Sydney's car last fall."

Sydney was his wife, and I remembered how they'd struggled to pay for car repairs the year before. That memory didn't exactly cheer me up.

"I've got to get back out there with these salads." He put the tray on his shoulder, heading for the swinging doors that connected the kitchen to the dining area out front. "But keep your chin up, okay? These things have a way of working themselves out."

I forced a smile onto my face as Greg disappeared through the swinging doors. He was only trying to help. It wasn't his fault that the only news was bad news. I placed the situation in God's hands. I had to trust Him to make a way for me.

Glancing at the clock overhead, I saw that my break was almost up. I finished my diet soda and was almost ready to toss the empty can into the trash. My boss, Holly, charged into the kitchen holding a clipboard in her hands.

"Kimmie, you're just the person I want to see." Holly swung her sleek auburn hair over her shoulder.

I'd always been intimidated by her. She was a serious professional and hard to please—not to mention a perfectionist about everything connected with food service.

"Can I help you with something?" I wiped my hands nervously on the skirt of my uniform, instantly self-conscious of my size sixteen figure compared to Holly's trim size six.

"That depends." Holly leaned back against a cabinet. "Are you free the evening of February 14?"

I swallowed back a laugh. Of course, I was free. I'd never had a date on Valentine's Day in my entire boring life. But I wasn't about to blurt that out to Holly. "Maybe," I said, keeping my face blank. "Why do you ask?"

"Worthington's is providing desserts for the charity auction to benefit the community center. Local merchants will be offering goods and services for auction, plus there's going to be a bachelorette auction for the finale. It'll be great free advertising for the restaurant."

Holly's eyes met mine, and she paused for a minute before continuing. "Everyone else has plans for Valentine's Day, Kimmie. You'd be doing all of us a huge favor if you agree to handle the dessert table. Think of the new customers this might bring in. That means more tips for you and Greg and the others. Plus, I'll pay you time and a half."

How could I say no? The extra cash could help me to pay for repairs to keep my car going. It seemed like the answer to my prayers. "Sure, I'll do it."

"Perfect." Holly glanced down at the clipboard in her hand. "You'll need to be here at around four o'clock to pick up the table, the linens, centerpiece, and desserts. We're preparing an extra large version of everyone's favorite."

"The chocolate almond cake," I mumbled to myself. It was the most expensive dessert on the menu, but it sold out almost every night.

"That's right." She glanced up at me. "You'll have sole responsibility for setting everything up and serving the guests. Are you sure you're up for this?"

I wasn't sure about anything, but I nodded my head in agreement. "I'll do my very best."

"Great." Holly turned and headed for the swinging doors before turning back to look at me over her shoulder. "And by the way, Kimmie. . . ."

"Yes?"

"You'll have to dress a little more, I don't know—sexy." She looked me over from head to toe with a critical expression. I felt the beginnings of a blush stealing across my face. "Try a shorter skirt, some high heels. There'll be plenty of single men at this auction, and we want to attract new customers."

Me . . . trying to attract male customers? I thought. If I hadn't needed the money so desperately to fix my car, I would've caught up with Holly and backed out. But I couldn't. I had to see it through.

Around four in the afternoon on Valentine's Day, I teetered out of the restaurant wearing a short black skirt and white blouse, along with makeup and black high-heeled shoes—just as Holly had asked. Luckily, I kept my makeup bag stocked for special occasions that rarely happened. The high heels and the skirt had been in my closet. The shoes had never been worn, and a price tag still hung from the skirt. Despite how silly I felt, I put them on. I knew everyone would laugh at me behind my back, thinking I was a fool for trying to pass myself off as attractive at my size.

Thankfully, I had the use of the restaurant's catering van for the night. My car had gotten worse every night, and I'd been catching rides to work and back with other members of the restaurant staff, hoping to spare any needless wear and tear on my vehicle until I could pay for repairs.

One by one, I carefully loaded the assortment of desserts into the back of the van, along with a folding table and tablecloth, and a gorgeous floral centerpiece Holly had splurged on to add color to the dessert table. Holly was usually the most frugal person alive, so I knew this event had a lot riding on it. I felt shaky and nervous just thinking about it, because it seemed as if the success of the restaurant were resting on my shoulders.

Driving to the community center, I turned on the radio to keep me company, but quickly turned it off again. Nothing but love songs, I thought. As if all the lonely people in the world needed a reminder that it was the night for romance.

There was very little traffic, so I arrived at the center within minutes, easily pulling the van into a parking space near the back entrance.

I climbed down from the driver's seat, tugging my short skirt down with a scowl. I headed for the back of the van and took out the folding table and cloth before making my way into the center.

Within minutes, I'd set up my table. I couldn't help but notice the dim, romantic lighting they'd set up, and the striking red foil hearts hanging on streamers from the ceiling. Clusters of Valentine balloons filled every nook and cranny of the place. It was like stepping inside a greeting card.

My heart ached with the pain of being alone on such a special night. A lump formed in my throat when I imagined couples lining the dance floor on the opposite side of the room. I'd never danced with any guy who wasn't related to me, and it stung my soul like a thousand wasps. I could picture the man of my dreams putting his arms around me, leading me out to the dance floor. "They're playing our song," he'd say, and I'd melt against him, wondering if heaven itself could be any more wonderful.

If only. I let out a long sigh. It was just a dream, one I had to keep in check if I was going to get through the night. I shook off the cloud of sadness hanging over me and set up the table, then went back outside to the van.

The table being set up, I went to work on bringing in the smallest items first: boxes of beautifully decorated cookies and tarts filled with fruit and cream. After taking those in and arranging them on the table, I went back out to get the larger items: two exquisite small cakes, and a huge chocolate almond sheet cake that was the highlight of our menu.

I leaned into the back of the van, and I carefully arranged the three cakes on the tray Holly had provided. I think I must have been holding my breath the entire time.

Stepping back carefully, I balanced the tray in my hands. I raised one foot to push the back door of the van shut, just as a car roared into the space beside me.

Those high heels—the ones I hadn't wanted to wear—betrayed me. As I nudged the door of the van shut, I lost my footing. In a moment that seemed like one of those slow motion instant replays, the three beautiful cakes went sliding off the tray, crashing down onto the pavement.

My eyes could scarcely believe what was before them. The cakes were smashed into a million crumbs at my feet. I tossed the tray aside and knelt down to pick up what was left of them, but I knew it was too late. They couldn't be salvaged.

I would be lucky if Holly didn't fire me. I briefly wondered if I could get away with serving just the cookies and tarts. Would Holly have to find out about this disaster?

As I sifted crumbled cake through my fingers, the sound of a car door slamming beside me registered somewhere in my frenzied thoughts. A deep, masculine voice addressed me. "Is there anything I can do to help?"

I didn't bother to look up. "No, it's ruined. I'm going to be in so much trouble." Tears burned behind my eyelids, threatening to destroy my carefully applied eyeliner and mascara.

"Trouble? Why?" The guy from the car knelt down on the pavement across from me. "No use crying over spilled cake."

His laugh was warm as it rolled across me. "Or is it spilled milk? Either way, don't cry. It can be fixed."

I finally raised my eyes to look at him. Even through my haze of tears, his good looks rendered me breathless. With his tall, athletic build, dark blond hair, and baby blue eyes, he could have easily posed as the man of my dreams.

And there I was: my extra pounds crammed into a short skirt, sitting on a mountain of cake crumbs!

I felt ridiculous.

I stood up so fast it made me dizzy. "I, uh . . ." The guy had me stammering. "I have to call my boss."

I left the cake for ant food, and I walked to the center as fast as those horrid high heels would carry me.

"Wait!" I could hear him calling after me. "You didn't tell me your name!"

I didn't look back. There was no need to tell him my name, since it was about to be mud.

Holly slammed the strawberry pie down on the dessert table. "That's the last of them."

I hung my head. I'd come clean with Holly, taking full responsibility for the loss of the cakes. I knew I had to be honest—no matter what the truth cost me.

She reacted with fury over the phone, but she'd brought down every last dessert from the kitchen. They weren't special items like the cakes I'd dropped. But, combined with the cookies and tarts I'd managed to bring in, there was enough of our usual fare to cover for my accident.

"Make no mistake, Kimmie." Holly glared at me. "This is coming out of your paycheck. The first round of desserts, plus these replacements."

I looked at the trio of fruit pies and the coconut cake Holly had brought, mentally adding them to the tally of desserts I'd ruined. It would cost not only the overtime I'd hoped to make, but also a sizeable chunk of my regular paycheck.

My heart sank. I knew this meant the end of my plans to repair my car. I'd have to rely on friends for a ride, or spend all my extra money for the bus.

Watching Holly stomp out of the community center, I'd never felt like such a failure. And to make matters worse, the great looking guy from the parking lot walked in just as Holly walked out.

I wondered if it would be too crazy for me to hide under the table. I couldn't meet his eyes, even though I felt him looking at me.

"Hey, it's you." A sunny smile lit up his face, making him look even more incredible. "Looks like you were able to come up with some more treats." He leaned down to examine a peach pie. "I could really go for a slice of this."

77

I cut a triangle of peach pie and placed it on a plate, handing it to him without a word.

"Say, I was wondering if—" He paused, as if he were searching for the right words.

Just then, the auctioneer banged his gavel down on the podium at the front of the room, and he began to thank everyone for supporting the community center.

"Listen, I need to get to my seat, but I'd like to talk to you later. All right?"

I must've nodded, but I was too hypnotized by his sexy blue eyes to know for sure. He took a seat near the dance floor, leaving me to wonder if the evening could get any worse.

The auction was in full swing, and desserts were practically flying off the table. I'd watched auctions for spa days at beauty salons, baskets of makeup, dog grooming, and every other service imaginable.

Lost in my own misery, I hardly noticed when bidding opened for a tune-up provided by Marvin Brady of Top Job Auto Care.

I glanced up at the proceedings, and I saw the guy from the parking lot standing by the podium.

My stomach rolled over a few times. He's a mechanic? Instead of dropping cake at his feet, I should have asked for his opinion about my car, I thought.

Naturally, the women in the audience weren't about to let a chance to spend time with someone like Marvin Brady get away without a fight. The first bidder—a thin, attractive brunette, upped the price by fifteen dollars.

A redhead on the other side of the room raised it by twenty-five dollars. After that, there was no stopping them. After much screaming, the first bidder won. I watched her sashay up to the podium to get her certificate, flashing Marvin a Cheshire cat grin.

I sighed, and wished I could take one of the fruit pies outside and comfort myself with it. Food had never let me down. It was always there when I needed it. And did I ever need!

Trying to ignore the beginning of the bachelorette auction, I cut myself a sliver of pie and tried to eat it without calling much attention to myself. But it was impossible not to notice how thin and pretty the bachelorettes were, and how crazy the men were for them. They cheered and applauded heartily for each woman, paying outrageous sums of money for a night on the town with one.

Sure, it was for a great cause, but nights on the town were probably commonplace for most of those ladies. For me, it would have been like living out a fairy tale.

The auction was coming to an end, and my feet hurt so much that the only thing I could think about was getting back home to soak in a hot bath. I'd been standing the entire time, serving desserts, smiling on the outside, while inside, I was in a fever over the mess I'd found myself in.

The auctioneer thanked the audience for their generosity. I packed the leftovers to drop off at the homeless shelter on the way back to the restaurant. Going back to Worthington's and facing Holly seemed about as appealing as root canal, but I had to do it. No use crying over spilled cake, as Marvin had said.

I put the box of leftovers aside and began to remove the centerpiece from the table, half listening to the auctioneer's announcement about the dance to follow the auction.

Wonderful; just what I didn't need. Having to watch everyone pair off and hit the dance floor would be the worst way to end a bad day. I tore the cloth from the table and shoved it on top of the box, determined to get out of there before I could be the only girl without a date—again.

I folded the table with a bang. Balancing it up against the wall, I saw Marvin Brady standing a few feet away, his eyes focused on me. I turned my back to him. I knew he felt sorry for me—the poor clumsy fat girl, spilling cake all over the place like an idiot. I didn't want sympathy. It made me feel even worse.

Thinking better of my earlier decision to toss the tablecloth aside, I reached down, picking it up to fold it. Holly appreciated neatness, and I was determined to do whatever it took to hold on to my job. It was then that I realized Marvin had gone up to the podium and was having a heated conversation with the auctioneer.

I watched them gesturing back and forth to each other, then gasped when they both turned to look at me. What on earth? . . .

The auctioneer took the microphone in his hand. "Ladies and gentleman, may I have your attention?"

The hum of chatter in the room came to a dead stop. Marvin's sparkling eyes met mine, sending butterflies through my stomach. I had no idea what they were about to do, but I knew it had something to do with me.

"We've had a most unusual request, but since it's all for a good cause, we ask for your patience."

These words from the auctioneer were met with surprised murmurs from the crowd. Every face in the center turned toward him expectantly.

"We thought our bachelorette auction was concluded. But it seems we have one last gentleman ready to bid on the lady of his choice." The auctioneer turned to Marvin. "Mr. Brady, when you're ready."

Marvin's blue eyes bored into mine. "I'm willing to match tonight's top bid for a date with the young lady behind the dessert table."

All the air rushed out of my lungs, the full impact of his words sinking in. Every eye in the place focused on me.

I felt dizzy, almost faint. A million thoughts raced through my mind, but one broke through the finish line.

He felt sorry for me.

The crowd began to chant excitedly for me to go up to the front of the room and join Marvin. A furious blush heated my face, and my hands began to shake. I couldn't do it. I couldn't go up there and call attention to my shame—the lonely, plus-sized waitress, pitied by the handsome mechanic for all to see.

And just when it seemed that my humiliation was complete, an older man who'd come back for multiple servings of pie removed a thoroughly chomped cigar from his mouth and piped up. "I'll raise you fifty." He laughed. "I always did like 'em full figured."

Hot tears stung my eyes. Why did Marvin do this to me? Why couldn't he see that I just wanted to stay in the background, invisible to the criticism and judgment of others?

A woman standing nearby grabbed me by the arm. "Go on up front," she hissed in my ear. "Are you going to let the kids who depend on this center down?"

I wanted to disappear, to dissolve into the floor and never be seen by human eyes again. Going up to the front of the room and standing under that bright spotlight was a scene straight out of my worst nightmares.

But the woman was right. I couldn't let the kids down. Too many people depended on the community center to provide a safe place for their children to go after school. I had to go up to the front of the room and face my shame. Otherwise, I couldn't live with myself.

I wiped my eyes with the back of my hand, and I walked on those dreadful high heels to the podium, through the rowdy crowd, past all the hands that reached out to pat me on the back as I passed by.

When I finally reached the podium, the auctioneer shouted the dollar amount of Marvin's last bid and asked if anyone would go higher. The older man with the cigar shook his head, bowing out of the bidding.

"Going once," the auctioneer cried out. Marvin reached out and tried to take my hand, but I snatched it away from him. Embarrassment had left me too raw to be touched.

"Going twice. Going three times." Silence met the final call for bids. My eyes squeezed shut against the scalding spotlight and tears streamed unchecked down my face. I'd never been so ashamed. I'd become a pity project for a handsome bachelor.

The gavel came down with a bang that made me flinch. "Sold! To Mr. Marvin Brady."

I rushed out of the center with all my stuff tucked under my arm and made it to the van before anyone could stop me. Opening the door so hard it nearly came off the hinges, I threw everything into the back. Nothing mattered anymore but getting out of there as quickly as possible. I had to salvage whatever dignity I had left.

"Hey, wait up!"

I didn't have to look behind me to know Marvin had followed me. I slammed the van door so hard the entire vehicle shook.

"Haven't you done enough for one night?" I crossed my arms over my chest in a defensive stance, my pain becoming anger.

Marvin raised his eyebrows. "What are you saying? That it was wrong for me to want to spend an evening with a beautiful woman and help a good cause?"

Beautiful woman? Had anyone ever said those words to me before? "I thought you acted out of pity for me." I heard a note of softness creeping into my voice.

This guy had a way about him.

He laughed. "I felt pretty sorry your cakes were ruined. I'll admit that. But why else would I feel sorry for the prettiest girl at the Valentine's Day dance?"

It was too good to be true. Things like that didn't happen to girls like me. They were reserved for the beautiful size fours of the world. "You're just saying that to make me feel better." I leaned back against the van, exhaling painfully. "Why would you want to be with me, when you could have had any one of the girls in the auction, tonight?"

"Because," he reached across and put a warm hand on my arm, sending shivers down every inch of my skin. "You're everything I've been looking for." His hand moved down and found mine. "Curvy, sexy, beautiful. . . ." He squeezed my hand for emphasis. "And real."

A happiness like none I'd ever known swept through me. "I don't have any night on the town planned for you. In fact, I'm flat broke, I may be out of a job tomorrow, and my car is going down for the count."

He threw his head back and laughed. "After bidding on you, I'm broke, too. But I think I can probably help you with your car." He put his arm around me and drew me closer. For the first time in my life, I didn't pull away to hide my extra pounds. I knew I'd found someone who liked me for myself—full figure included.

"What do you say we go back inside and have one dance before the night is done?" His eyes sparkled down at me.

It was an offer I couldn't refuse. Still holding his hand, I let him lead me back inside the center. Before we reached the door, he turned to me with a smile. "Feel like grabbing a bite after the dance?"

Did I ever. "As long as it's not cake!"

Needless to say, I got my car fixed, thanks to help from my own personal mechanic. And I guess you could say I learned to like cake again. Marvin and I plan to have one at our wedding in a few months. But you can bet it won't be chocolate almond!

I never thought something like this could happen to me. I believed that dreams were for other people, that love would never find me. But I was wrong.

God's ways are a mystery to us. Being sold at auction was the last thing I expected, but it brought me the love of my life. I learned to love myself, too.

Marvin may have been the highest bidder that night, but I'm the one who walked away with the prize!

The End

STORMY LOVE
How A Hurricane Changed My Life

"**Y**ou need to come on home," Mom said. "I don't want you caught in this horrible storm."

I'd just moved from Ohio to Pensacola, Florida, a couple of months earlier, and Mom called me nonstop with worry. It was my first time away from my hometown. Sure, I was homesick, but I still wanted to assert my independence.

"I'm fine," I said. "Really. Stop worrying."

I heard her sigh.

"Elise, promise you'll leave if it looks like it'll hit Pensacola."

"Okay, okay, I promise. I'm sure everything will be just fine. All my neighbors have been through this, and they tell me it's no big deal."

After I got off the phone, I turned around and visually scanned the room. As meager as it was, everything in the apartment was all mine. I'd scrimped and saved for almost every item, from the lumpy couch I'd picked up at a thrift store, to the cheap knickknacks on the shelf made of particle board.

I grabbed the remote and flipped on the tiny TV that my grandmother had given me for my birthday when I was still in high school. The news was on, so I flipped it right back off. Okay, so a hurricane was coming. Did that mean nothing else was going on? I wanted to watch my favorite show, but they kept interrupting it with reports about this stupid Hurricane Ivan.

Since I'd never been through a hurricane before, all I could go by were accounts of other people's experiences and what I'd seen on the news. From what I could tell, most places didn't get much damage. The people who had the most to worry about were those who lived on the beach—and my place was a couple of miles from the beach. Sure, I knew I'd get some wind, but my building had survived other storms—and it was still standing.

I puttered around my apartment for a few minutes, until I heard the doorbell. It was my neighbor.

"I just heard we have a mandatory evacuation," he said. "We have to get out of here."

"What's that supposed to mean?" I asked, annoyed that anyone would even think of telling me what to do.

"It means they think Hurricane Ivan is gonna hit Pensacola, and they don't want us here."

I planted my fist on my hip and tilted my head to one side as I glared at him.

"Where are we supposed to go?"

"The high school. That's one of the shelters."

I snorted.

"The high school? What are we supposed to do there?" I paused for a moment before adding: "Pack in like sardines with a couple hundred other people who are scared of their own shadow? No thanks."

I knew I sounded sarcastic, but really. . . .

He shook his head.

"Look, I'm not trying to start an argument, but if the storm does hit, we could be in big trouble. I just wanted to let you know."

"Okay, thanks. Consider me warned."

My neighbor walked away toward his own apartment, while I stood there watching—wondering what to do. On the one hand, I was a little afraid, but on the other hand, I was not gullible when it came to sensationalistic news hype. The media people were always thinking of an angle to sell advertising, so they built things way out of proportion.

As the day wore on, weather conditions progressively deteriorated. The sky that had been blue with fluffy white clouds had turned a light shade of gray, and the wind had kicked up several notches. Intermittent rain showers sprinkled the roof, and occasionally when I looked outside, it was moving horizontally—meaning the wind velocity had increased.

I felt a prickle of fear on my skin. Even now, with the storm still hours away, I was scared. I didn't like the sound of the loose gutters banging on the side of the building. The howling of the wind through the gutters had the eerie sound of someone blowing into a soda bottle. Debris flew by, and loose garbage cans skittered across the apartment complex—creating a loud clanging sound that added to the noise.

Another couple of hours passed, bringing even stronger winds. Every once in a while, I glanced outside and spotted another resident of my apartment complex evacuating, luggage and bottles of water in hand. If this continued, I'd be the only person left in the building. Fear gripped me as my imagination took over. What if the wind or water was as bad as they feared, and my building blew away? I wasn't ready to die.

Acting quickly, I pulled my biggest suitcase out from beneath my bed. The people on the news had said that shelters would fill up fast, and once they reached capacity, they'd have to turn people away. They also said that each person could take only one piece of luggage.

I ran around my apartment gathering up the few possessions I owned that meant anything to me—pictures, documents, personal items, and a few articles of clothing. I'd forgotten to buy extra water before the stores had run out, so the only thing I got out of the kitchen was a big pack of stale peanut butter crackers.

By the time I had everything together, the wind was howling, and the rain pounded against the windowpane. I started to open my door, but the gust of wind blew a picture off my wall and nearly knocked me over. I leaned against the door to close it. No way could I even think about driving to a shelter in this kind of weather.

Now, fear gripped me harder than ever. This storm was as bad as everyone had said it would be. I shuddered; then, I thought about how I had to find a way out.

Picking up the phone, hoping for the phone line to still work, I listened for the dial tone. Good! There was one. I'd heard that some storms were so bad, they knocked out phone lines.

I punched in the emergency number and waited. Finally, after almost a dozen rings, someone came on the line.

"I'm stuck in my apartment and can't get out," I said.

My voice shook in spite of the fact that I was trying to remain calm.

"Ma'am, can you give me your exact location?" the man said.

I stated my address and asked when they could have someone out to pick me up. He started to talk; then, the line went dead.

"Hello?" I said, frantically. "Hello? Anyone there?"

It quickly became apparent that the phone had gone dead. The lines were down. Now what?

By now, the apartment building shook with each new gust of wind. The rain pelted the window so hard I couldn't see the parking lot. I just knew I was going to be trapped in this apartment—and if it blew away, I'd be dead.

I didn't think it was possible for it to get any worse, but it did. The sound of the wind was sort of like that of a train approaching a railroad crossing. The rain hit the windows with such a force, I was certain they'd crack. Why hadn't I gotten out like I'd been told?

My insides tensed as I gathered up some pillows, and hovered in the hallway between the living room and my bedroom. It was the only place without windows, so I figured it was probably the safest spot to be. I crouched on the floor with a couple of pillows over my head, praying that the storm would end soon.

Then, after what seemed like forever, I heard a loud banging at my door. At first, I thought it was the wind, but then I heard my name.

"Ms. Kirby!" I heard. "Elise Kirby, are you in there?"

My eyes widened. The man's voice bellowed, and under any other circumstances, it would have frightened me half to death. But this was one time I was glad someone I didn't know was at my door.

I ran toward the door and turned the knob. Then, the door flew open from the force of the wind, and its force knocked me over. A man wearing a yellow slicker rushed inside, and put all his weight against the door to close it.

"Why are you still here?" he asked. I couldn't see his face very well because his slicker was the kind with a hood, and he had his face buried in the bottom part that had been buttoned all the way to the top.

"I—I. . . ." I began, then my teeth started chattering from fear.

The wind continued to howl.

"It's not gonna get any better," the man said. "We have to leave. I probably should have left you here, but when you told me where you were, I figured I needed to come and get you before the storm surge."

I'd heard about storm surges, before. That was when the water from the Gulf came up and swallowed land and everything in its path.

"Take my hand," he instructed me. "We can't stay here another minute. I got one of the firemen to take a truck, so we'll have to make a run for it."

I nodded and did as I was told. As brave as I'd tried to be, that was all over—now that I'd seen firsthand how bad a hurricane could be. And to think the worst of it wasn't even here yet! I couldn't imagine.

The trip to his truck was . . . a real trip. We leaned into the wind as it blew in our faces, but then once in a while, it changed direction. Somehow, my rescuer had the ability to anticipate the change, and he never failed to catch me before I fell. I knew I was in good hands.

The fireman drove us through whipping rain and wind, through the streets of Pensacola, all the way to a school. When we pulled up in front of the building, he nodded toward the door.

"Get out here, and go on inside. I'll be there in just a minute."

I managed to get inside fairly easily because the building provided a small shield from the driving wind and rain. I stood at the entrance, watching and waiting for the man who'd saved me. I still didn't know what he looked like.

However, I did recognize the yellow slicker that had ripped on one side when he'd caught me. He stepped inside, shrugged out of his slicker, and shook his hair, sending drops of water flying. When he stopped, stood still, and turned my way, my heart pounded. Not only was he big and strong, he had the most gorgeous, deep brown eyes I'd ever seen in my entire life. Our gazes met in what seemed like a random magical moment that had nothing to do with the storm. In fact, there was a brief flash of time when I actually forgot about what had brought me here.

"You okay?" he asked, breaking the silence.

I opened my mouth, but nothing would come out. So I clamped my mouth shut, swallowed hard, and nodded. He raked me with his gaze, sending goose bumps down my spine—in a good way. There

86

was definitely some chemistry happening between us.

Finally, he took a step back and said, "Look, I gotta run. Do me a favor and stick around until this thing blows over."

"Don't worry," I said, softly, "I'll stay."

The worry lines around his eyes softened. I could tell he really cared.

A woman from the shelter came up from behind and gently guided me further into the building.

"Chester's a good boy," she said.

"Who?"

I looked at her and saw the sweet smile on her face.

"Chester. The EMT. The man who brought you here."

"His name is Chester?" I thought for a moment and tried to remember if he'd told me his name. He hadn't. "Yes, he's very nice." With killer eyes and a drop-dead gorgeous smile that turned my knees to rubber, but I couldn't tell her that.

"He's one of my favorites," she said with a nod. "He cares about others more than himself. He's saved many lives."

Although I knew I'd be eternally grateful for what Chester had done for me, what she said filled me with sadness. As bad as it sounds, I wanted him to feel that special something I felt when we looked into each other's eyes.

"Would you like some coffee, dear?" she asked as she guided me to a chair. "You certainly look like you could use some."

"Uh, yes, that would be nice," I replied.

"Cream? Sugar?"

"Yes, both please."

She left me alone for a moment while she got my coffee. That gave me some time to regain my composure.

"Here you go, honey. I hope I fixed it to your liking." She sat in the chair next to me.

"Do you work here?" I asked.

We were in a school cafeteria that had been designated a storm shelter.

"I used to be a cafeteria worker, here; but I'm retired now. That gives me time to lend a hand during disasters."

"Oh," I said, before I took a sip of coffee. It felt so nice and warm going down. That was comforting, because I felt lost and scared. Alone.

"Tell me about yourself, dear," she said. "Where are you from?"

Over the next hour, I learned that her name was Grace, and she'd been widowed for two years. She had two grown children: a son who was a few years older than me, and a daughter who was my age. That was why she seemed to instinctively know just the right words to comfort me. I felt a connection—like she was standing in for my mom.

I had my back to the door, so when her gaze was averted, I spun around to see what she was looking at. There were three EMT's standing in the doorway, looking around the room—now half filled with evacuees. Grace lifted her hand and wiggled her fingers in a wave. Chester pulled away from his friends and made a beeline toward us. My heart pounded.

"We've decided to ride out the storm here," he said. "It's getting too dangerous for anyone to be out there, although I feel bad if someone needs us."

Grace patted his hand.

"Sometimes, you have to think of yourself, Chester." She stood up. "Stay here with Elise while I go see about that boy over there."

"Sure thing," Chester said.

I sat there staring after Grace as she walked away. Silence fell between Chester and me as my mind raced with all sorts of thoughts. My attraction to Chester was overshadowed by the fear that I wouldn't have a home to go to after the storm.

Suddenly, something hit the side of the building, and the place quickly grew quiet. I froze.

"Are you okay?" Chester said, as he leaned toward me.

"How long is this gonna last?" I asked.

He shrugged.

"Hours. I'm not sure how many."

"Will this place be okay?"

He nodded. "It's built to withstand hurricane force winds," he replied.

Then, he reached out and took my hand as he looked at me with a questioning glance.

I accepted his gesture with gratitude. It was nice having someone there beside me, even though I knew he was too charming and handsome to feel anything for me.

"Do you have family in this area?" he asked.

I shook my head.

"No, they're all in Ohio."

"I bet they're worried about you," he said. "In fact, I heard the storm is being shown live on the national cable networks."

"Oh, that's just great," I said. "My mom's worried enough about me. She so doesn't need to watch it happen."

Chester laughed.

"We've become a nation of news junkies. And it's almost like watching a movie. I wonder if people think about the reality of the lives of those who actually go through it."

"I doubt it," I replied, "except my mother. She knows."

"After the storm, the cell phone towers will be down until they get crews in to bring them back up," he said. "But I have a phone you can use to let your parents know you're okay."

The way he looked at me caused my heart to do one of those flippy things. I offered a shaky smile. "Thanks."

The storm grew stronger and much louder, sending debris flying into the side of the building—the sound echoing through the large cafeteria. I felt fear like I'd never felt before. Finally, after several hours of the worst part, Chester stood up and stretched. "Sounds like the worst is over. I need to get out there and see if anyone needs me."

My heart ached at the thought of him leaving me.

"Are you coming back?"

He looked down at me, tenderness evident in his expression.

"Do you want me to?"

I nodded without a second of hesitation.

"Yes."

With a grin, he nodded.

"I'll come back for you after I check out the area. Promise you won't leave until I get back."

I laughed.

"I don't have any way of getting home, so I don't exactly have a choice."

The second he left, I looked at the clock. Time dragged by. Chester was gone exactly seven hours and fifty-three minutes.

When I saw his face at the door, my heart beat in double time. He zoomed in on me and was by my side in a flash.

"Your place held up pretty well," he said. "I drove by and checked, just in case I needed to warn you."

I let out a sigh of relief.

"Thanks so much. I don't know how I can thank you for all you've done."

"Well," he said, slowly as he studied my face, "there is one thing."

I licked my lips.

"What's that?"

"You can go out to dinner with me next Friday night."

"I'd love to," I said.

From our first date on, I knew I was in love with Chester. Five months later, he asked what I'd like to do for Valentine's Day, since it was quickly approaching.

"Surprise me," I said.

His eyes twinkled as he nodded.

"Sounds like a good idea. I'll totally surprise you."

He told me to wear my prettiest dress, so I chose a sexy red dress that I thought was perfect for Valentine's Day. I wore simple silver drop earrings and a watch.

When I opened the door to Chester, his appreciative gaze let me know I'd picked the perfect outfit. "You're gorgeous," he said.

I giggled like a teenager.

"Thank you, Chester. You look nice, too.

He wore a gray suit with a dark red tie. I'd never seen him so dressed up, but he looked fabulous.

We went to a nice restaurant on the other side of town—which I thought was the big surprise.

"You couldn't have picked a nicer surprise," I said.

"This is only the beginning," he said as he wiggled his eyebrows.

"What else can you possibly have up your sleeve?"

He looked up his sleeve and winked.

"There's something else up there. Just hang on, baby, and you'll see."

After dinner, he took me to a play sponsored by the community theatre group. It was a humorous production that had been written specifically for Valentine's Day. I laughed until I thought my sides would split.

"I'm having the best time," I announced as we left the theatre.

"It's not over, yet." Suddenly, he grew quiet and pensive. I looked at his face and realized something had instantly changed about him. It wasn't bad; it was just different.

He drove out to the beach. I inhaled deeply, taking in the scents of the Gulf of Mexico. I loved Pensacola when it wasn't storming.

"Let's get out," he said. "It's a little chilly, so I brought a blanket."

He wrapped us up together in the blanket. We walked over toward one of the benches and sat down.

"This is the most wonderful evening of my life," I told him. "Thank you so much for giving it to me."

Chester stared out at the water as it lapped the shore. Then, he turned to me and swallowed hard. "There's something else," he said. Then, he wiggled a little until he was out from under the blanket. He reached in his pocket, got down on one knee, and opened his hand. On his shaky palm was a sparkling diamond ring, glistening in the moonlight. "Will you marry me, Elise? I want every night to be as special as this one. I'll do everything in my power to make you happy."

Speechless, all I could do was nod. He slipped the ring on the finger I offered, then cupped my chin in his hand. When he kissed me, I felt a rush of love so strong, I would have fallen over if he hadn't been there, holding onto me.

"To think, this all started with a storm," I finally managed to say. "Hurricanes can be so scary, but with you by my side, I'll always feel safe."

We got married the following summer. Since my apartment was so small, I moved into the house he was renting. It was nice and perfect for the two of us.

"Hurricane season's about to rev up," he told me one afternoon when he came home from work. "There's a tropical system brewing out there, and there's some concern we might get hit, again."

I smiled.

"But you'll protect me, right?"

"I'll do my best." He gave me a squeeze. "But it could mean longer hours for a few days."

I'd always known he had to work during emergency situations; so I nodded. However, that didn't keep the dread from washing over me.

We watched the news and weather reports on TV as Hurricane Katrina did her wild thing, dipping down on the southern tip of Florida, before heading north in the Gulf of Mexico.

"She can hit anywhere," he said. "The only thing we're certain of is that she'll make landfall somewhere on the Gulf Coast."

"What are the chances of her hitting Pensacola?" I asked.

He tilted his head, thought for a moment, then shrugged. "At this point, it's too hard to tell."

As Katrina made her way north, we saw that she was unpredictable. Then, she made a jog to the west. I let out a sigh of relief. Chester looked worried.

"This is not a good thing," he said. "If she hits New Orleans, the whole country is in a heap of trouble."

He explained how New Orleans was mostly below sea level and how the entire city could flood. The whole country also depended on imports, exports, and the oil industry supplied by that region.

"I'd like to help out if they get hit," he said.

My husband's kindness, generosity, and helping nature were the very things that had made me fall in love with him to begin with, so I nodded.

"I'd like to help, too."

He hugged me and said we'd help whoever needed it. Then, we watched and waited as Katrina made landfall in one of the worst possible places.

Because roads were blocked at first, we had to wait three days to head over to the Mississippi area. We'd been advised to stay out of New Orleans, so we decided to bring needed supplies and food to people in Biloxi and Gulfport. People from our church donated a truckload of items as well as cash.

The devastation was apparent right away. My heart ached as I realized how dire the situation was.

When Chester pulled up in front of one of the few structures standing, I took one look around, sucked in a breath, and got out.

"I think this is the shelter they wanted us to bring stuff to," he said.

We went inside the building with one of the guys to help us unload the truck. The truck was empty an hour later, and the people in the building had food, diapers, personal hygiene products, and toys.

I noticed one of the emergency workers hovering over a young woman who appeared to be slightly younger than me. When I had a chance, I asked him if she was his wife or girlfriend, and he shook his head.

"No, I just met her when she came here."

I cast a quick glance over at Chester, who winked and pulled the guy aside. As they chatted, I saw a smile on the man's face, and he nodded. Chester reached into his pocket, pulled out a pen and slip of paper, and wrote something down. He handed it to the man. Then, Chester came over to me and said, "Let's go. They have enough stuff for the next few days."

On the way back to Pensacola, I turned to my husband.

"What did you tell that emergency worker?" I asked.

He laughed.

"I told him how we met. He said the second he saw that woman, he felt an incredible urge to protect her."

"Then what did you say?"

"I told him to wait until Valentine's Day to propose!"

"What did you write on that paper?" I asked.

"Our names and phone number. I told him we want to come to the wedding. . . ."

The End

REALITY ROMANCE
Behind The Scenes Of A Reality TV Show

The man's voice on the phone asked, "Ava Ingram, please?"

"This is Ava." My heart raced.

The man sounded exactly like the announcer on my favorite reality TV series, Get a Job.

"This is Warren Wagner with Get a Job. Congratulations! You've been selected to be one of twelve contestants on next season's show."

I let out a shrill scream, sending the entire IT department into my office area.

"This is Warren Wagner with Get a Job. Congratulations! You've been selected to be one of twelve contestants on next season's show."

I let out a shrill scream, sending the entire IT department into my office area.

"What happened, Ava?" Brent from the cubicle next to mine said.

After hyperventilating for several minutes, I informed all the wide-eyed people standing around what had just happened. "Can you believe my luck? They actually wanted me."

"You're kidding, right?" Elijah asked. "This is a joke."

"No joke," I said, unable to keep myself from grinning ear to ear.

"When you told us about trying out," Brent said, shaking his head, "I never expected it to actually happen. Well, I'm certainly happy for you."

"Thanks, Brent," I said, still feeling giddy with delight. My feet hadn't touched the floor since the call.

As they went back to their desks, I overheard one of the guys say, "I bet someone's playing a practical joke on Ava. Stuff like this just doesn't happen to people like us."

"Don't listen to 'em," Caren, the only other female in the department, said. "They're just jealous."

My confirmation letter, instructions, and contract arrived in the mail two weeks later. I'd already requested an indefinite leave of absence, and it had been granted. I worked for a very progressive company. Most of my coworkers were young and really got a kick out of reality TV. They now believed me, and they were proud of me. And I had no doubt they were about to enjoy some reflected celebrity status once the shows aired.

"You do realize it'll be dog eat dog, right?" Caren said over lunch one day.

"Of course, I do. But take a look around. You and I are the only women in this crazy office, and we've survived. How much more difficult can being on that show be?"

"For one thing," she said, "millions of people will be watching. There's some pressure in that."

"I'll be fine," I said with a flick of the wrist. "And, I think, I stand an excellent chance of winning."

Caren tilted her head to one side, studied me for a minute, then grinned. "Ya know something, Ava? I think you're right. You're as smart and shrewd as any guy out there."

"Thanks," I said, feeling great about having someone in my life who believed in me—other than my family.

I still had several months to go before taping of the show started, and they seemed to drag. But finally, the time had come for me to leave my job and head out for a whole new adventure.

"We love you, Ava," Caren said as she gave me a big hug.

"You'd better win, girl." Brent hugged me and gave me a gentle shove toward the airport terminal. As I walked away from the small group who'd come to see me off, he hollered, "You're doing what we all wish we could do. We're counting on you."

I boarded the plane, fastened my seatbelt, and let out a huge sigh. What I was about to embark on was scary, exhilarating, and totally crazy.

Warren Wagner had told me I'd be rooming with one other young professional woman, but each week things could change, depending on who was let go and who was left.

When I got to baggage claim, I was greeted by a man wearing a chauffeur's uniform. He informed me that my luggage would be taken care of, and he whisked me off in one of the limos waiting at the arrival gate. I felt like a big celebrity. Then it dawned on me. I was a celebrity—or would be as soon as the show aired. My heart hammered, and my face felt flushed. Soon, people would know me by sight, and my name would become a household word among fans of Get a Job.

Since my accommodations had been taken care of by the show staff, I didn't have to bother with check-in. All I had to do was ride up the elevator to my room. The bellman slid in his key and gestured for me to go first.

I walked inside and found myself face to face with a snarling, long-nailed, overly made- up, hard-edged woman. She towered over me and I gulped.

"You must be Ava," she said in a sarcastic tone.

"Uh, yeah," I replied. "Sorry, but I don't know your name."

She tossed a snarky grin and rolled her eyes. "You'll find out soon enough."

Okay, so she wasn't going to tell me her name. And she obviously had no intention of even trying to be nice. I knew we were in direct competition, but this was ridiculous. Every show I'd watched the prior season, had friendships and interactions between the contestants.

Then I remembered they also had at least one person on the show who appeared evil—the villain. As I looked at my roommate, I realized I'd been stuck with that person.

Oh, man, why does this have to happen to me?

Since I knew better than to fight the woman on her terms, I just shrugged. "Whatever," I said. "Doesn't matter to me, anyway."

She planted her fist on her hip. "Trust me, sweetie," she said, her eyes narrowed, and her lips tight over her teeth. "It'll matter to you very soon. I plan to walk away with the grand prize, and I don't care what anyone does; no one will stop me."

I couldn't help but laugh out loud. This woman was playing her part to the hilt—maybe even being overdramatic.

"Only fools laugh at me," she said. "And you'll regret it."

Trying to disguise my shaky breath, I crossed the room to open the curtains. It was dark in the room, adding to the creepiness of being alone with this woman.

"What are you doing?" she asked.

"Letting in some light," I replied, forcing myself not to look her in the eye.

"I like it dark. Close 'em back."

"Nope," I said as cheerfully as I possibly could. "They're staying open."

She started to say something, but a loud knock came at the door. "Cameramen," someone called.

"Lights, camera, action," the woman snarled. "Go open the door."

As much as I hated taking orders, I decided to be the good roommate. I opened the door and greeted the three people standing there. One person had a still camera, the other had a camera on a wheeled stand, and the third person had a clipboard.

"You must be Ava," the guy with the clipboard said. "And I presume that's Sydney."

I glanced over my shoulder, grinned, and said, "Nice to meet you, Sydney."

She glared back at me. I heard a whirring sound and turned to see that the camera had started rolling.

Okay, so this is where the show gets interesting, I thought. I needed to play up this interaction and let Sydney's snotty side really show. She obviously wanted to be the villain, and I was getting paid to be here, so I decided to taunt her a little.

"Sydney, why don't you take the bed closer to the window? It'll be

95

nice to get that sunshine on your face every morning."

Was that fire I saw in her eyes?

"I just love bright, cheerful rooms," I said, making sure the camera caught my good side, knowing I sounded like a Pollyanna. I walked back over to the window and yanked the curtains open a little wider. "Don't you?"

"Close those curtains," she growled.

I cast a quick glance at the cameraman who was grinning and giving the thumbs-up sign. He was getting the footage he needed.

"Oh, no, I can't do that. How do you expect me to see?"

She threw her bag onto her bed—the one farthest from the window—and she stormed over to where I stood. Before I had a chance to move, she yanked the curtain from my hand, nearly knocking me over in the process, and pulled the curtains shut.

"If you open them again, you'll be sorry," she said.

The cameraman lowered the camera and backed toward the door. "Perfect. Just what we needed." He and the other guys were at the door when he paused and added: "You ladies have fun. We'll be seeing a lot of each other."

After they left, she grabbed her bag and started ranting. "I never should have agreed to do this stupid show! If it weren't for the prize, I would have told them right where they could shove it."

"Oh, Sydney, relax," I said. "It's all what you make of it. If you want to have fun, you will. Don't be such a grouch."

Her eyebrows shot up. "You ain't seen nothin' yet, babe. I'll make your life miserable. That's what I do best."

No doubt she would, too. I let out an audible sigh. "Suit yourself. I plan on having a great time."

"You're a fool," she said.

We spent the next hour unpacking in silence. I could tell I didn't need to push Sydney any further than I already had. People like her had short fuses, and I wouldn't put anything past her. Then I wondered if rooming with her was safe.

That night, during dinner, I met the rest of the contestants. There were six women and six men, all of them hungry for the grand prize. Since this was the third show with a similar basic format, I knew it wouldn't be nearly as popular as the first with curious viewers wanting to see Donald Trump in action. However, the prize was just as good: a year's worth of capital for a startup business of our own. Besides, we were all getting free room and board, nice perks at the corporate office, and a small salary—which was close to what I made on my regular job.

"Hey, Ava."

The guy sitting across the table from me had been staring at me for several minutes, but I'd been deep in thought until he said my name. I looked at him and saw his handsome face crinkling as he smiled at me.

"Yes?" What was his name? I couldn't remember it to save my life.

"You seem to have a great outlook on life," he said. "I like that in a woman."

"I try to be positive," I admitted. "No point in being down all the time."

"You have a pretty smile."

I took a long, hard look at this guy. Was he sweet-talking me for a reason, or was he just being nice?

The expression on his face was one of kindness and sincerity. Although I wasn't sure about anything, I would have been willing to bet he was just being pleasant.

"Thank-you," I said. "So what do you do for a living . . . well, before this?"

"I'd just joined an investment firm."

"So you're a stockbroker?" I asked.

He lifted his shoulders and let them drop. "Sort of. I will be after I finish my training. How about you?"

"I work . . . worked in an IT department at a retail company."

"Sounds interesting," he said. "How long have you been there?"

We chatted for a while about our jobs. Then he looked up and had a surprised expression on his face. I looked around and discovered we were alone.

"I wonder where everyone went," I said.

Behind a cupped hand, he pointed to the corner of the now-darkened room, where the camera people were aiming their equipment right at us. "Don't look now," he said, "but I think we're being filmed."

I snickered. "I forgot all about that. This is so insane, being filmed all the time. I wonder if they'll ever give us any privacy."

"I doubt it," he replied. "But we knew that coming into it, right?"

With a gulp, I nodded.

He stood and I followed. "I'll walk you to your room. We have a long day tomorrow."

Both of us tried to pretend we weren't aware of the cameras behind us as we headed to the elevator. They hung back as we got on the next elevator, but when we got off, they got off another elevator, going in a different direction. Then we walked down the long corridor to my room, not saying a word. I imagined that they'd probably play music on the show and make it seem like I was taking him back to my room with me. Now I wondered about the romantic couple on the previous season's show and wondered how much of their relationship was real.

He stood at my door for a moment, then chucked my chin. "Have a nice night, Ava. See you in the morning."

I couldn't help but look to see if the camera was on us. They were gone, to my disappointment. I wanted them to see me go into my room—by myself.

Once in the dark room, I tiptoed so I wouldn't wake my roommate. But she let me know she wasn't asleep.

"What were you and Bernard getting all worked up over?" she asked sarcastically.

Bernard! That was his name.

"We were just talking," I said.

"You were undressing each other with your eyes, that's what you were doing."

"Oh, get over it, Sydney. You'll never get a guy with your attitude. Didn't your mother ever teach you that you catch more flies with honey than with vinegar?"

"First of all, I don't want a guy. Secondly, I don't even know my mother. And last, only someone like you would think catching flies is a good thing."

I grunted. This woman was totally impossible, but maybe she'd just explained her problem.

"I'm really sorry about your mother," I said.

"My mother?"

"Yes, you said you don't know her. I'm sorry. My mother and I are very close."

"Why am I not surprised?" she said. "I lied when I said I didn't know my mother. I do know her. I just don't like her."

"I'm sorry about that, too."

"You're an idiot, Ava," she said. "That's why you won't last a week on this show. The rest of us will eat you alive."

I sniffed. "We'll just have to see about that, won't we?"

After silence fell between us, I allowed myself to think about Bernard. He was one of the sweetest guys I'd ever met. If I wasn't careful, I knew I could fall for him. He was exactly what I wanted in a guy.

The next morning, we met in the hotel lobby, where Kyle Pantalone, the owner of the show, waited with his entourage. I looked around, hoping for a glimpse of Warren Wagner, the announcer, but I didn't see him.

"I hope you all got a good night's sleep," Kyle said, "because we're gonna hit the ground running today. I have an assignment ready as soon as we form teams. Take a look around. I'll pick team captains, and you can take turns picking who you want on your team."

I nodded as I glanced at everyone, sizing them up, trying to decide who'd be good to work with and who wouldn't. The only person I didn't want, for sure, was my roommate. And one person I did want was Bernard.

Kyle lifted his hand and pointed his finger at me. "Ava, you'll be captain of the blue team." I gasped as I realized what this meant. It was my responsibility to pick who was most likely to win, so we wouldn't have to kick someone off. The losing team had to dump one person each week, until half of the group was gone. Then, Kyle would pick who left the show each week.

Then, Kyle moved to the other side of the group, sizing up everyone. He stopped by Bernard, looked away, then turned to face him. "And Bernard, you'll be the green team captain."

My heart sank. There went my chance of being on a team with the one person with whom I felt most comfortable. Oh well. This would only be for two weeks. Then we'd start mixing it up again and literally start over with new teams.

Since I got to go first, I quickly picked a woman who'd been somewhat friendly during dinner the night before. I figured the best strategy in the beginning was to find people I could work with. Their job skills would show up soon enough.

Then, it was Bernard's turn. He looked over the group, took a quick glance at me, and to my surprise, he chose Sydney. What was he thinking? Maybe I'd been wrong about him. Did he like her more than he'd let on?

With a smirk, she sauntered over to his side, getting way too close for my comfort. I felt my heart lurch as I realized she was cozying up to him to get to me. I looked away. Letting her see my discomfort would only feed her evil side.

After we chose teams, we were told to go ahead and meet with our groups in one of the two hotel restaurants. I did my best to avoid Bernard, but he caught up to me and tapped me on the arm. I turned to face him.

"I didn't want you to have to deal with her in the first go-round," he explained. I knew he was talking about Sydney. "I took her off your hands so you could relax."

"You did that for me?" I asked, somewhat doubtful.

"Yes. It's really obvious she's jealous of you, and she'll do anything she can to hurt you. I wanted to keep her from getting you off to a bad start."

I started to smile, then I remembered this was a competition among all of the contestants—including Bernard and me.

"Thanks," I said, "but you don't have to worry about me in the future. I'm perfectly capable of taking care of myself."

An extremely confused expression crossed his face. "But—"

"Hey, it's cool. Don't worry about it. Have fun." With that, I turned and walked away from him, leaving him to wonder.

All day, as my team planned our strategy, Bernard was in the back of my mind. What was he doing? Was he getting close to Sydney? Did I upset him and make him want to side with Sydney in getting rid of me?

That night, exhausted, I returned to my room. Sydney wasn't in yet, so I had the bathroom to myself. After a long, hot bubble bath, I got into bed. She arrived just a few minutes after I'd turned off the light.

"I know you're not asleep," she said as she went through the room turning on all the lights.

"Turn off the light," I said.

"No. I can't see in the dark."

"I thought vampires could see in the dark."

"Very good, Miss Ava. You catch on quick." She flipped on the TV, then plopped down on the edge of the bed. "I guess you want a play-by-play of your boyfriend's activities today."

"Not really. I don't have a boyfriend."

"Could've fooled me. I saw how you were looking at Bernard. Besides, he's hot!"

I sighed. It looked like I was in for a long night of her taunting and annoying behavior.

"Did you plan your week?" I asked.

She rolled her eyes. "What do you think? Duh."

So much for a decent conversation with this evil monster. I groaned, sank further beneath the covers, and pulled the blanket over my head.

The next morning, Bernard was at the elevator when I got there. "I've been waiting for you," he said. "Wanna join me for breakfast?"

"Shouldn't you be with your team?" I asked.

"Probably. But I'd rather eat with you."

We got on the elevator and rode down in silence. When we got to the lobby, no one from the show was in sight. "Okay, I guess we can have breakfast since no one else is here."

I didn't say much at first, but within a few minutes, I felt myself warm up to Bernard. He truly was a nice person. He even had me laughing.

Then suddenly, his expression changed. He looked mortified.

"What?" I asked.

"Look behind you, off to your right," he whispered.

I quickly glanced around and saw the cameramen, their equipment aimed at us again. "They're filming us?"

"Looks like it. They really don't miss a beat, do they?"

"I guess it makes for a more interesting show," I agreed. "I wonder what they'll keep and what they'll cut."

"I have a feeling you and I might be stars of this show," he said.

"And I suspect Kyle picked us to be team leaders because he saw us talking and thought it would be a good hook."

"No doubt," I said.

"Wanna give them something to really get worked up over?" he asked as he scooted his chair around closer to me.

"Sure," I replied, my heart racing at his closeness.

Next thing I knew, he'd cupped my head in his hand and pulled my face toward his. As his lips covered mine, I thought I'd this must be what heaven feels like. This man was not only heart-stoppingly gorgeous; he was the best kisser in the universe.

As we pulled apart, he gazed into my eyes with a dopey look on his face. "Ava. . . . " Then he didn't say anything else. He didn't have to. Both of us knew something was happening between us.

Later that day, as my team finished our plans to present to Kyle, I avoided anywhere I thought the other team might be. Seeing Bernard would be entirely too distracting, and I couldn't afford messing up my big chance at this awesome opportunity.

Kyle approved our plan and gave us the money we'd put in our budget. Then we set out to start everything in motion. The instant I walked outside the hotel doors, I ran smack dab into Sydney.

"What'd you do to our leader, Ava?" she asked. "He's been acting weird and jumpy all day."

"Nothing," I said. I didn't owe her any explanations, especially about my relationship with Bernard.

"Just remember he's your opponent. Anything that happens between you and him can only work against you."

"Mind your own business, Sydney," I said. I knew better than to think she was actually trying to help me.

"I'm just warning you." Then she turned the corner and left me in her dust.

Somehow, I managed to finish my first task. Again, I got back to the room before Sydney, who did a repeat performance of the night before. Only this time, I'd removed some of the light bulbs from the fixtures, leaving only one by the door.

"I'm on to you," she said as she slammed the door shut. "Bernard told me about your little scheme."

Now she had my attention. "Scheme? What scheme?"

"Oh, don't play stupid, you little twit. Bernard told me how you have it out for the other women on the show, and you'll do anything to get rid of us."

"Come on, Sydney," I said with a groan. "Can't you think of something better than that."

She cackled. "Don't tell me you think that kiss was anything more than a ploy to get information out of you."

I sat up in bed. "He told you that?"

"That and more," she replied. "Much, much more. Good night, Ava darling." Then she turned off the light and disappeared into the bathroom.

The next morning, Bernard was waiting for me again. I wasn't sure what to do or how to act around him, after what Sydney had said.

"Are you okay?" he asked.

"Fine," I snapped.

"Okay, I give up. What did she say?" he asked. "I know something's up."

I had two choices: give him the silent treatment or confront the issue. Since I've always been above-board in all my relationships, I decided to tell him.

After I explained what had happened the night before, he shook his head. "Don't you understand what she's doing to you? She's trying to psyche you out. Don't listen to a word she says. You can't trust that woman a single bit."

He was right. I finally nodded and told him the pressure of the show had knocked a little sense out of me, but he'd just knocked it right back. He laughed.

"One of the things I like about you is your interesting and completely different way of seeing things," he said.

I felt my heart thump harder as we exchanged a look of understanding. I needed to be careful, or I'd fall deeply in love with this guy who seemed to be able to read me better than anyone I'd ever known.

The rest of the week was pretty much the same, but I didn't let my roommate affect me like she had in the beginning. Finally, the week ended, and the final tally showed that my team won. Kyle had to choose someone to let go from his team. I fully expected it to be Sydney, but he chose one of the guys, instead.

"I don't get it," I said later in the bar. "Why would you keep someone as evil as Sydney?"

He shrugged. "They wouldn't let me get rid of her."

"Who wouldn't?" I asked.

Bernard glanced over at the door, then shook his head. "I can't say."

I started to look over my shoulder, but he whispered, "Don't turn around. They're watching."

Okay, now I get it. The people from the show—the producers— want to keep Sydney on the show. That makes sense. Since they brought her to the show for her evil side, they want to keep her around for conflict.

The following week, Sydney was one of the team leaders, and one of the very weakest guys was the other. This had to be some sort of warped strategy to keep ratings high, but it was also annoying.

I sat and watched as Sydney's gaze scanned the group of us. For a moment, I was certain she'd pick Bernard, but then she looked past him, then at me, her lips forming a smirk.

She lifted her finger, arched one eyebrow, and said, "Come on, Ava. You're on my team."

I couldn't think of a worse nightmare. As it was, I was stuck with her as a roommate—at least until one of us was eliminated. Now I had to hang out with her all day for a whole week. Ugh.

On her next pick, I was shocked again when she chose Bernard. I'd assumed she'd pick one or the other of us—but not both.

Later on, as we huddled together in the hotel coffee shop to discuss strategy, her rationale dawned on me. She wanted to keep her eye on both of us for some strange reason.

As the week went on, it became painfully obvious that Sydney was trying to throw the contest. She did everything in her power to make our team lose. Bernard had a theory.

"I think she wants to eliminate one of us," he said.

"But why?"

He shrugged. "She's jealous, I think."

Bernard and I vowed to work hard to win, but we lost by quite a bit. Sydney was called to the producer's office, and when she came back an hour later, she scowled at us.

"I was hoping to get rid of you, Ava," she admitted, "but they told me you had to stay. I just don't get what's going on. Those people are as stupid as the rest of you."

When I told Bernard, he nodded. "That's what happened when I wanted to get rid of Sydney. They asked me who I thought was the weakest person on the team, and I said Sydney. They said they needed her on the show. And now, it's obvious you and I are attracted to each other, so they probably want to keep us around for the romance element."

He had a good point. I just sat there and sipped my diet soda, letting this whole thing sink in. When I'd watched the show as an innocent viewer, I had no idea all this behind-the-scenes stuff was going on. It should have been obvious, now that I looked back.

During the next six weeks, we lost person after person, until we were whittled down to a very small group of four. Then the rules changed. It was two and two.

"He's only using you, ya know," Sydney said one night as we got ready for bed.

"Come on, Sydney, stop it. You're such a troublemaker."

She paused, holding up her brush and staring at me, then she spoke. "You can't be that naïve, Ava. Bernard is a snake in the grass. Don't tell me you don't notice how he's always in view of the camera. And when you have an idea, he adds just enough to it to make it his own. That man will do anything to win this competition."

"That's ridiculous," I snapped.

After we turned off the lights, and I heard her soft snore, I lay there thinking about all the things she'd said. As much as I didn't want to believe her, she was right about some of it. Bernard did always manage to be in front of the camera. He had a way of speaking to people when they were the most dramatic and showing his diplomatic side. And he always came across as the wise one in the group—the one who could settle differences and calm people down.

Then Kyle Pantalone, the owner, was the one who picked each person to let go. Drama was high, and nerves were on edge as we watched people we liked leave.

One day, after a really intense day of frazzled nerves and hot tempers flaring, Bernard pulled me to one side and said, "Ava, I'm crazy about you."

"What?" His timing was totally off. We were about to go into the deepest and most intense part of the competition, and he was telling me he was crazy about me?

"I want us to have a relationship," he said. "You and me."

"You and me?" I repeated, my voice cracking.

"Yeah," he said with a nod. "As in really romantically involved—not just for the show."

Remembering what Sydney had said, I glanced around to see if there was a camera focused on us. I didn't see one.

"Really?" I asked.

He took my hand in his and nodded, grinning ear to ear. "Really. I've fallen in love with you." His look of self-confidence bothered me. Why was he acting so sure of himself?

"Is this for the show?" I asked.

"The show?" Now it was his turn to act perplexed.

"Yeah. The ratings," I replied.

Bernard closed his eyes but didn't let go of my hand. When he opened his eyes, he pulled me closer, gave me a gentle hug, then took a step back.

"I really do love you, Ava. I tried to keep it from happening, but I can't help it. It has nothing to do with the show, except that I met you here."

I swallowed hard. He sure did seem sincere. Oh, what the heck. I'd fallen in love with him weeks earlier, so what did I have to lose? "I love you too, Kyle."

He blew out a sigh of relief. "I was hoping you'd say that."

"But what now?"

Bernard shrugged. "I'm not sure yet. We need to talk about this later. I just needed to get that straight with you before we went on to the next phase of the competition."

The next day, we were interviewed by a television entertainment show. They were mostly interested in Bernard and how he was so diplomatic and Sydney because she was so vicious.

"I guess that's why I've been so successful in business and now on this show," Bernard said.

"Smug jerk," Sydney mumbled.

"He's right," I said. "His diplomacy does help in business."

"Like I told you," Sydney whispered, "he's a snake in the grass."

I felt an odd tingling sensation as he glanced over toward me and winked. Sydney noticed it, too, and she snorted.

"Stupid girl," she said.

"I'm not stupid," I said in my own defense. "Bernard and I just happen to be in love."

"If you really believe that, I have some swampland for sale."

When Sydney had her turn in the interview, she snarled and made rude comments, clearly giving the interviewer exactly what he'd expected. My interview was the shortest of all.

Then, after I'd joined the other contestants, the host got our attention when he turned to Bernard and asked, "Is it true that you've become romantically involved with one of the other competitors?"

Bernard hesitated just long enough to make me wonder if maybe Sydney was right. Then he shrugged. "That's really not anyone else's business. If you're asking how it'll affect me on this show, I can assure you that I can separate all personal and business relationships--without any problem."

"See?" Sydney said with a smug smirk. "What'd I tell ya?"

I felt my heart sink. Maybe she was right. If he really did love me, wouldn't he want to shout it to the world?

After the news people left, Bernard came toward me with a look of determination.

Sydney leaned over and whispered, "Don't let him get away with dissing you. That's how women get hurt."

In spite of how much I didn't trust Sydney, I couldn't take the chance of getting hurt on national TV. Before Bernard reached me, I turned and walked away, leaving him in my dust. When I glanced over my shoulder, he was standing there, looking dejected. Serves him right, I thought. But deep down, I hated doing that to him. What if Sydney was wrong?

That night, Sydney was nicer to me than she'd ever been before. She even tried to make me feel better about myself by saying Bernard didn't deserve me.

Naturally, I was miserable, but I managed to pour myself into the show, doing everything possible to stay in the competition. It was down to Sydney, Bernard, a guy named Craig, and me. I could tell Sydney was pretty sure of herself, but that was expected. Bernard and Craig had never gotten along very well, probably because Craig was a male version of Sydney.

We were preparing to go into the very last phase of the show, when Sydney and I both were called down to the lobby of the hotel for an emergency meeting. When we arrived, Craig was there, but Bernard wasn't.

"Where's Bernard?" Sydney asked.

"Unfortunately, he left the show," Kyle said. "We thought about bringing one person back, but we've decided to let one of the episodes go through two weeks. That'll build drama and help you get your plans together a little better. Remember, now you're on your own."

"I wonder why he left," I said. "Did he tell you?"

"No," Kyle replied as he squinted his eyes at me. Something was up.

Sydney snorted. "He couldn't take the heat."

During the next week, I had a horrible, sick feeling in the pit of my stomach. I'd almost forgotten what time of year it was, until my mom called to wish me a happy Valentine's Day.

"I know it's not until next week," she said, "but I was afraid you'd be too busy to talk to me then."

"Thanks, Mom," I said. "This show is taking a lot out of me. I'm beginning to wonder if it's worth all this."

"Sure it is, honey. If anyone can do it, you can."

After we got off the phone, I was even more miserable than before she called. Now I was reminded that the only guy I'd ever told I loved was no longer in my life. Bernard was everything I'd ever wanted in a man, and now he was gone.

"Oh, stop your sniveling," Sydney said. "You'll get over it. Men like Bernard are a dime a dozen."

"Just leave me alone," I said. "You don't know anything about men."

She opened her mouth, then clamped it shut. For the first time since I'd known her, I'd gotten the last word in.

On the morning of Valentine's Day, I noticed that Kyle, Warren, and all the production people were walking around with goofy grins on their faces. "What's up with them?" Sydney asked.

"Who knows?" I replied. "Maybe they've got big plans with their sweethearts tonight."

"Oh, give me a break," she said sarcastically. "All they care about is ratings."

About a half hour before we were due to go down to the lobby of the hotel for a quick makeup job, I got a call. It was one of the makeup people.

"Mind if I come up and do yours now?" she asked.

I glanced over my shoulder. "Uh, I guess that would be fine."

"I'll be there in five minutes."

When the knock came at the door, Sydney let Carol in. "Wanna do mine first?" Sydney asked.

"No," Carol said, brushing right past Sydney. "You go downstairs."

"But I thought—" Sydney said.

Carol shrugged. "Boss's orders. You go to the usual place, and I do Ava here."

"But why?" I asked.

"Who knows? I'm only taking orders."

Sydney shot me a suspicious look. "I'm leaving," she said. "I can't stand to watch this."

After she was gone, I turned to Carol. "Really, why are you here? I could have come down."

"I just want to make sure you look perfect," she replied, now relaxed and smiling.

"I must be getting the ax," I said as I settled back in the desk chair. "You don't have to bother with waterproof mascara. I won't cry."

"Oh, you might," she said as she pulled a long tube from her bag. "I'm putting waterproof everything on you, tonight."

"Whatever," I said with a flick of my wrist. "Let's just get this over with."

When she was finished, I was startled at the way I looked. My makeup was way more than professional. I was downright glamorous looking.

She crossed over to my closet and started thumbing through my clothes before she stopped and pulled out a cocktail dress. "Wear this," she said.

"I was going to wear my black suit with the teal camisole," I argued.

"No," she insisted. "Wear this."

"But why?" I asked.

"Trust me. You'll be glad you did."

After she left, I started to put on my black suit, in spite of the order she'd given. However, I figured there must be a reason I needed to wear the dress, so I followed her orders. Although I felt ridiculous leaving my room in the dress and wearing way more makeup than I usually wore, no one could accuse me of not going along with the producers' whims.

When I reached the lobby, I could tell something was different.

The lighting was low, and tiny white twinkle lights had been strung through the small trees and plants in the lobby. Huge red hearts on lacy backdrops were suspended from the ceiling, reminding me it was Valentine's Day.

Then suddenly, the crowd parted, making an aisle for me. I glanced nervously around at the faces that held a secret I couldn't even try to guess.

When Bernard stepped out of the crowd, right in front of me, I blinked. Was I hallucinating? He'd left the show a couple of weeks ago. He wasn't even supposed to be here.

"Ava," he whispered softly as he took my hand. "Do you trust me?"

I frowned as I studied his expression, one of honesty and genuine concern. Then I nodded. "Yes, I trust you."

He cleared his throat and turned me toward him. "Ava, I have a confession to make. I wasn't able to remain on the show, competing with you, with my feelings as deep as they are. I went to Kyle and the producers who understood my feelings."

I looked up to where the show's executives stood, watching, waiting in anticipation. Kyle nodded and smiled, gesturing toward Bernard.

"Ava, I'd like to ask you a very important question," he said as he dipped his hand into his pocket and pulled it back out, his fist tightly closed as if he was holding the most valuable possession in the world.

"A question?" I asked.

Bernard got down on one knee, then opened his hand, allowing me to see the shiniest diamond ring I've ever seen in my life. "Will you be my wife?"

My heart must have stopped and started a dozen times before I could catch my breath. Wha—?"

I heard several gasps from the crowd, letting me know I'd heard right. My hands shook as my mind raced.

"Please," he whispered. "If you say yes, I'll be the happiest man in the world."

"Well," I said as I regained some of my composure, "this is Valentine's Day, and I do love you." After a brief pause, I nodded, with tears streaming down my face. "Yes, I'll marry you."

Suddenly, everyone broke into applause. Bernard stood back up, scooped me into his arms, and planted a huge kiss on my lips.

After the magic of the moment, we were all ushered into the smaller of the two hotel restaurants, where several large, round tables were waiting for us.

Sydney wouldn't look me in the eye. Instead, she scowled at Bernard as if he'd done something to hurt her intentionally.

As we sat down, Bernard leaned over and whispered, "I wanted to do this privately, but they talked me into doing it on the show. I figured that would be okay with you, since we met here anyway."

"It's fine with me," I replied. "It'll save me the trouble of having to call everyone I know."

We had a wonderful dinner, then Bernard and I went for a walk so we could be alone. He explained how he'd been working with the producers since he'd left, getting this whole thing coordinated.

"They even want us to have a televised wedding," he added.

"What did you tell them?" I asked.

He shrugged. "I said it was up to you."

"Well," I began slowly. "It would be okay if that's what you really want. But I'd much rather have a more private ceremony."

"I was hoping you'd say that," he said. "We'll just send them wedding pictures."

That night, when I got back to the room, Sydney was gone, and she'd removed all her things. I called down to the lobby and learned she'd left the show. Now, it was just Craig and me.

Since I had something much more important than the show to think about, my heart wasn't in the competition. It was no surprise that Craig walked away the winner. But I felt that I'd won the grand prize. I'd fallen in love with the most wonderful man in the world, and we were getting married soon.

According to Kyle Pantalone, Bernard's proposal was the highlight of the season. "We're thinking about doing a dating reality show next," he admitted. "Get a Job has run its course, and quite honestly, it's hard to compete with Donald Trump. Not all the stations picked us up for another season, unless we could guarantee something to top your engagement." He lifted a shoulder, then let it drop. "I don't suppose I could talk you into letting us televise your wedding?"

"Not a chance," I replied.

He snickered. "Oh well, that's show business. At least we're ending it on a good note."

Everyone, including my parents and all my friends from work said my relationship with Bernard was the highlight of the show. And with a twinkle in her eye, my mom said, "This was the most romantic Valentine's Day I've ever seen."

Those were my thoughts exactly. And a year later, it's still true!

The End

AN AFFAIR TO FORGET
Is Heartbreak The Next Step?

I was concentrating so much on what I was doing that I didn't hear his footsteps.

"Hey, Mom! What're you doing?"

I jumped a foot into the air at the sound of Nathan so close behind me. Hastily, I shoved the half-wrapped paperweight—shaped like a lighthouse—behind the toaster. Hopefully, it would be out of sight.

Too late.

Nathan had seen it. With the curiosity of a teen, he reached around and pulled it back into full view.

I bit my lip as his brow rose. Without a doubt, an endless stream of questions would follow.

Too late.

Nathan had seen it. With the curiosity of a teen, he reached around and pulled it back into full view.

I bit my lip as his brow rose. Without a doubt, an endless stream of questions would follow.

He fingered the figurine, drawing my attention to the fact that his nails needed trimming. "That's neat. Is it someone's birthday?"

Birthday? I pounced on the excuse. "Yes, yes. It's my secret pal's birthday." More like someone I secretly admired, and it definitely wasn't his birthday, I thought.

"Who's your secret pal?" Nathan persisted.

Oh, why oh why couldn't my son—for once in his life—behave like a normal teenager and not care about anyone but himself? I was immediately ashamed of my thought. I was lucky Nathan was so sensitive and caring, and I knew it.

"If I told you, I'd have to kill you," I joked, nervously.

Nathan snorted. "It's not like I would tell anyone. The only friends you have are the friends you work with at the warehouse, and you never invite anyone over. You should get a boyfriend, you know."

Shock thrummed through my face at his unexpected words. I found myself on the verge of blurting out the truth, but I decided against it. What would I say? That I had a crush on a guy I wasn't sure even knew I existed? Just the thought made me flush with embarrassment. It sounded so immature that I knew that I couldn't say anything to my son . . . yet.

I could, however, remain hopeful that someday, soon, I'd be able to tell him something.

"I have to get to work," I said. "And you'd better get to school. If you're late again, you'll have to stay after school."

"Why are you going to work so early?" Nathan asked. He looked at the kitchen clock and frowned. "In fact, I think this makes the second time this week you've left early. What's up?"

I groaned inwardly. Again, I didn't think teenagers were supposed to notice such mundane things about their parents. "Well, I . . . I . . .we're a little behind on shipping, so I've been going in early to catch up."

"Oh. That's right. Valentine's Day is coming up."

To my relief, Nathan grabbed his backpack and headed for the door without further questioning. I worked in the shipping department of a mail order catalog company, and Nathan knew that holidays were our busiest times.

The moment he was out of sight, I hastily finished wrapping the small gift and headed out the door. As I started my car, I punched in my best friend's phone number.

Tuesdai answered on the second ring, sounding breathless. Without saying hello, she said in a slightly grumpy tone, "I'm up and I'm ready, Brenna. Only for you would I go to that godforsaken place thirty minutes early."

I felt my face go warm all over as I backed out onto the street and began my trip. "I'm lucky, I know. I really do appreciate this, Tuesdai."

"I know you do. That's why I'm doing it." There was a pause, and then Tuesdai said cautiously, "I don't suppose you've changed your mind about asking him out?"

"No." I didn't hesitate.

After not dating for several years, I knew I'd never get the courage to ask Madison P. Carey out on a date. It was difficult enough to find the courage to spell out my name a letter at a time with each gift I left on his desk.

Today was the "N." Even without the "A," he would know my first name after today. The realization filled my stomach with butterflies.

We'd spoken, briefly, at the vending machines in the break room. I didn't even know if he knew who I was, so telling him my first name might still leave him clueless.

What if he doesn't care enough to find out? What if he finds out, sees me, and doesn't want to ask me out? I thought.

I knew there was a big possibility that I could get hurt, and that's what scared me the most. After my last disastrous relationship, I was understandably nervous about opening up my heart to a man again.

Tuesdai met me in the break room. Madison's office was in the warehouse in the basement of the big building. He worked in accounting, while Tuesdai and I worked with thirty others filling orders and packing the merchandise.

My hands were shaking when I handed her the wrapped paperweight. This was it, and I was terrified. My eyes must have looked huge, because Tuesdai gave me a hug before she tucked the package in the big purse slung over her shoulder.

"You're gorgeous, Brenna. He'd be a fool not to ask you out."

"I'm not gorgeous."

"Compared to the rest of us, you are." Tuesdai glanced at her watch. We both knew that Madison arrived promptly at eight o'clock every day.

He was very punctual, well-mannered, and good-looking in a reckless, bad boy kind of way. Although he'd only been with the company six months, the rumor was he was every bit as charming as he seemed.

"Are you sure you're getting it to the right office?" I asked my friend, anxiously.

Tuesdai let out a self-suffering sigh. "How many Madison P. Careys can there be?"

She did have a point, one that made me flush for being so silly.

"Actually, I think it's romantic," Tuesdai said, pausing at the door to flash me an encouraging smile. "Especially what you have planned for the letter."

"You don't think it's childish?" I held my breath as I waited for her to answer.

"No, I don't. I think it's wrong for women to assume that there isn't a man alive that would appreciate a dozen red roses and a box of chocolates. My bet's on Madison."

"I hope you're right." I cringed inwardly at the thought of my plan backfiring. What if Madison laughed at me to my face? What if he made fun of my romantic overtures? I knew that I would die on the spot if he did.

Today was Friday. Monday was Valentine's Day, and on Monday night the company was hosting a Valentine's Day party at a nice nightclub.

If Madison liked the roses and candy I was going to leave on his desk Monday morning, I was hoping he'd asked me to be his date for the party.

Tuesdai returned after about ten minutes, and we clocked in, and went to work. It wasn't until break time that I dared to think of Madison and his reaction to the lighthouse with the sentiment written in pink lipstick on the base. In fact, I was so engrossed in imagining his reaction that I didn't see the granola bar taped to the outside of my locker—until I was swinging the door open to get my purse.

I froze, staring at the chocolate chip oatmeal granola bar. It was the kind I ate from the vending machine most days during my break.

Slowly, with my heart beating nearly thudding out of my chest, I pulled it loose.

On the back, written with a red mark was the letter M.

It was from Madison. I guess he knew that I ate granola bars every day at break time. He knew, and he'd bought one for me.

My heart swelled with hope and joy. Madison knew who I was now, and he liked me.

Along with the joy came a rush of relief. The secretiveness was over. My crush was out in the open, and maybe, it was reciprocated.

My legs were weak as I retrieved a pop from the vending machine. Then I joined Tuesdai and a few others at one of the tables. I stared at the granola bar for a long time, and finally, decided I couldn't eat it. Like a giddy teenager with her first love, I wanted to save it. Maybe I would freeze it and give it back to Madison on our tenth wedding anniversary, to see if he remembered it.

"Earth to Brenna, earth to Brenna."

I looked up at Tuesdai and blushed at her amused expression. There, I was daydreaming about being married to Madison, and he hadn't even asked me out! I stuck the granola bar in my purse, and I tried to look innocent. For some reason, I didn't want to share my granola bar discovery with Tuesdai just yet. I wanted to savor it a little longer before she and I started analyzing it to death.

"Did you say something?" I asked Tuesdai.

Tuesdai rolled her eyes. "Yes, I did, and I'm not going to repeat it. It wasn't worth mentioning twice."

"Sorry. Guess my mind was elsewhere."

"Speaking of which . . ." Tuesdai lowered her voice and leaned close, darting a glance over my shoulder. "Madison just walked in with Marvin."

I stiffened, but I didn't dare look right away. Marvin was our supervisor, and he had been with the company only a few months longer than Madison. He was a great guy who had relocated to get over his ex-wife, so rumor had it.

But it wasn't Marvin who had me holding my breath—although he was good-looking enough to make my female coworkers sigh and stare.

"He's looking this way," Tuesdai said, barely moving her mouth. "Turn around and smile at him."

I put my hand in my purse to draw courage from the granola bar. Then I slowly turned.

My gaze met Marvin's first. I was a little startled when he winked and smiled at me. I smiled back, and then looked at Madison. To my disappointment, he'd already looked away. So much for eye contact, I thought, turning back to Tuesdai.

113

"If you ask me," Tuesdai said, "Marvin is not only better looking than Madison, but he's friendlier."

"Yeah. Maybe a little too friendly," I said, recalling that flirty wink he'd given me. "Besides, his wife left him. There's gotta be a reason."

Tuesdai's voice turned a little chilly as she said, "I've been married twice. The first one liked to push me around—which wasn't my fault. The second liked women…, which wasn't my fault."

I was immediately ashamed of my senseless comment. "I'm sorry, Tuesdai. You're right. Maybe it wasn't Marvin's fault at all. I had no business assuming something I don't know."

She relaxed, but continued to grumble. "You've been married before. You should know that sometimes, it just doesn't work out."

I winced inwardly, not for the first time wishing I had told Tuesdai the truth about Nathan and myself from the beginning.

The truth was I'd never been married—and Nathan wasn't my birth son—although I'd raised him since birth. He was my nephew. He'd been born two months early in the back of an ambulance while my sister, Sharene, lay dying from her injuries. There had been a seven-car pile-up on the interstate, and twenty people had died.

My parents and I hadn't even known my older sister was pregnant, and we'd never found out the father's identity. The only information we'd been able to obtain from the people who had lived in the same roach-infested apartment building was that she'd been seeing a guy she called Marv, but they hadn't seen him enough to describe more than his general features.

Wanting to give Nathan a life as normal as possible, my parents and I decided to let him believe that I was his mother, and that his father had deserted me when I found out I was pregnant. I planned to tell him when he was mature enough to handle the truth.

My parents had tried to convince me to let them raise him, but they were already in their early sixties and not in the best of health. I had come to them late in life, and I think it had drained the last of their reserves to raise me.

Finally, I'd gotten my way. They promised to help me in every way they could—and they had—right until the day my father suffered a fatal heart attack. Two weeks later, my mother had a stroke. She hung on, mostly bed-ridden, for another year before she passed.

I bit my tongue, knowing I couldn't tell Tuesdai something of this magnitude until Nathan himself knew. No way was I going to risk Nathan hearing it from someone else.

I took a sip of my soda before I murmured, "Of course, I know what it's like. I don't know what I was thinking."

"Odds are you probably weren't thinking," Tuesdai said in a sly voice. "You're becoming obsessed with our new accountant, my friend."

Maybe I was. That thought scared the heck out of me. Deliberately, I forced myself to remember my last disastrous relationship. I had known Tuesdai at the time—although we hadn't been close—so she knew about him.

"I just hope I'm not making another mistake, for Nathan's sake as well as my own."

Tuesdai snorted, disdainfully. "You're not the first woman to fall for a lying, cheating two-timing weasel, and you won't be the last, unfortunately. You had no way of knowing that he was lying to you about being divorced."

I blinked back humiliating tears. "Maybe, but when I think that he was with me when his wife went into labor. . . . I just get sick to my stomach."

"It wasn't your fault," Tuesdai stressed, slightly exasperated. "Even his wife didn't blame you, remember?"

"Still . . ." Still, it made me cautious and downright petrified of falling into the same humiliating trap I had fallen into before.

"Brenna, you know things about Madison Carey, even if you don't know really personal things. You know he's not married. Having a job like this, he couldn't hide that glaring fact. You know he's not gay, because he's already been seen with two or three different women."

My smile wobbled on my lips. I realized that Tuesdai didn't know the depths of my terror. "Not exactly a lot of information, considering the fantasies I've been having about this man."

Tuesdai reached across the table and closed a hand over my clenched fist. She squeezed hard, giving me a smile of encouragement that I desperately needed. "Live dangerously, Brenna. I've got your back."

"But you don't know any more about him than I do."

"Maybe not, but I have ways of finding out, if need be." She sat back with a smug smile. "When and if you get ready to hear the dirt on Madison, I'll find it."

The thought of invading Madison's privacy in such a way turned me off, but I had to admit it was comforting to know that I could find something out if I needed.

What happened later that evening almost made me forget about Madison entirely.

Marvin was waiting by my car for me at the end of my shift.

Not Madison, but Marvin.

I swallowed my disappointment and forced a polite smile to my face as I approached him. "Need a ride? Your house is in my direction, isn't it?"

His flashed his gorgeous white teeth at me. "It is, but I don't need a ride. I actually got to keep my car after the divorce," he added, ruefully.

115

Feeling suddenly awkward, I fiddled with my car keys and waited for Marvin to tell me what he wanted. He didn't beat around the bush.

"I want to go out with you," he stated, bluntly.

"Oh." I didn't know what to say. Heat rushed into my face. Marvin was nice, and I didn't want to hurt his feelings. Before I could articulate an excuse, he dropped a bombshell on me.

"It was the lighthouse that clenched it. How did you know that I collected them?" He threw his head back and laughed, and I couldn't help noticing how tanned and strong his throat looked with that Adam's apple bobbing up and down.

Then his words sank in.

I gasped and staggered backwards, catching the edge of my hood for balance. "Wh–what?" I blurted out in a squeaky voice.

His bold blue gaze heated. His voice dropped to a husky rumble. "Don't be coy, Brenna. You know exactly what I'm talking about. The homemade brownies . . . the lottery tickets . . . the seventeen-piece minitool set. I'm half in love with you, already."

My legs nearly buckled as I stammered, "But—but—"

"I just regret that we've wasted this much time. I've been going out of my mind wondering who you were and where you've been all my life."

Marvin unfolded his tall, lanky frame, and he stepped closer. If possible, his gaze heated another ten degrees.

I just about fainted. The realization was utterly, frighteningly clear.

Tuesdai had taken my gifts to the wrong man, and Marvin thought I had a crush on him! He had no idea that Madison was the target of my affection.

And I found that I couldn't just blurt out the truth. In fact, I found I couldn't say anything. I was—at the risk of using a cliché—speechless.

"I didn't realize you were so bashful," Marvin said softly, stroking my chin with his finger. He let out a sigh and shoved his hand in his pocket, as if he didn't trust himself.

I swallowed a huge lump in my throat and attempted to speak. My voice was croaky as I stammered, "I—I don't know what to say."

Marvin lifted a dark brow. "How about saying yes to the Valentine's Day dance on Monday night?"

When I didn't immediately answer, his gaze flickered with uncertainty. "Unless you've already got a date—in which case, I feel like a fool."

Now that I was fairly certain Madison wouldn't be asking me, I could say with total honesty, "No, I don't already have a date."

"So you'll be my date . . . my valentine? Is that too corny?" He flushed and looked away. "I'm sorry. My ex used to say I should have been a woman, that I'm a hopeless romantic and that turned women off."

His ex—in my book—was a fool, and I couldn't let Marvin believe for a moment that I agreed with her. "She didn't have any right speaking for all women, because I happen to like romantic men."

"You do?"

The hopeful note in his voice tugged at my heartstrings. I didn't have the heart to just blurt out that he was the wrong man. After the way I had inadvertently led him on, I knew it was my responsibility to let him down easy.

Coming to a decision, I said, "Yes, I do. And I'd love to be your date for the dance Monday night."

Marvin let out a sigh of relief, and he slapped his chest. His grin was rueful. "Whew! For a moment, I thought I had the wrong secret admirer."

When I blushed to the roots of my hair, he threw back his head again and laughed. "Don't be embarrassed! I've been on top of the world since I found the first gift on my desk."

A polite smile hid my inner disappointment as I stepped around him to unlock my car. "Well, I'll see you later."

"Yeah, see you later, Brenna."

As I got into my car and watched him saunter away, I was surprised to find myself ogling his cute behind. I felt confused. Didn't I have a crush on Madison? Then why was I looking at Marvin as if he were an interesting desert? Was I that fickle? I finally shook my head and put Marvin out of my mind. I couldn't wait to get home and call Tuesdai and tell her the terrible news. Maybe my friend would have some insight into what I should do to untangle this mess.

"I'm telling you, Brenna, I did not get the wrong office! I can read, for Pete's sake. The nameplate said Madison P. Carey."

Listening to the rising tone of Tuesdai's offended voice, I bit my lip. Tuesdai wasn't slow or blind. So what had happened? How could Marvin have gotten what was intended for Madison? And I knew from our conversation in the parking lot that it wasn't just one gift that had found its way into the wrong office, but all four of them.

"Okay, then. You took them to the right office, but somehow, they got to the wrong person. It doesn't matter how, now. What matters is what I'm going to do about it. How can I tell Marvin? He looked so . . ." I frowned, recalling the boyish excitement in his eyes. "Um, restored."

"Restored? Did you just say restored? Because if you did—as your friend—I have to tell you, it sounds like you're talking about a painting or something. What do you mean?"

"Restored . . . as if his confidence had been restored," I explained with faint exasperation.

Tuesdai was my friend. She was supposed to read my mind to some extent—or so I believed.

"I think his ex really beat him down, you know? And when he started getting all those mystery gifts . . . well, he started feeling better about himself again."

"Oh my God! I'm so glad you didn't take my naughty advice about that black leather men's thong." Tuesdai's tone sounded as if she was trying to smother a laugh, but she hadn't quite succeeded.

I didn't see what was so funny, and I shuddered at the memory of how close I had come to taking Tuesdai's more worldly advice.

"Never mind about how much worse it could have been. What should I do now?"

"God, I don't know, Brenna. Go out with Marvin?"

I swallowed an impatient sigh. Tuesdai wasn't normally so dense. "I have to go out with Marvin. I already promised him. I just don't know when I should tell him the truth."

"If you tell him before the dance, he'd probably let you off the hook."

Envisioning Marvin's acute disappointment and humiliation, I winced. The guy had obviously suffered a huge blow to his ego at the hands of his ex. What harm could it do to at least give him one good night before I told him? It wasn't as if I'd be dumping Marvin to go out with Madison, since it turned out that Madison didn't have a clue how I felt about him.

I'd have to start all over in that department . . . when I discovered how Tuesdai and I had managed to mess things up in the first place.

Saturday morning, I called the flower shop and canceled my Valentine's Day bouquet and candy. The woman informed me in a frosty tone that due to the late notice, my order would be charged to my credit card, anyway. With that in mind, I had the order sent to my home address instead. If I was going to have to pay for them anyway, I could darn well enjoy the flowers and the candy.

Saturday night, Nathan had a hockey game, so I didn't have much time to think about Madison or Marvin.

On Sunday, Nathan and I stuck to our routine: church, then lunch at a family restaurant that served good old-fashioned food. Over chicken and dressing, I told Nathan that I had a date for the Valentine's Day dance.

He feigned a heart attack, making me smile. "So who's the unlucky guy?"

I stuck out my tongue at him. "Very funny. Nobody you know. He works at the warehouse."

Nathan shoved a huge bite of green beans into his mouth. Then he continued to talk with his mouth full—despite the one million times I had asked him to refrain.

"I know just about everybody you work with," he pointed out. He swallowed hard, then he gulped a half a glass of sweetened iced tea as if he hadn't had anything to drink in days.

"He's one of our supervisors."

"Ohhhh." Nathan wiggled his brows comically. "One of the big guys, huh?"

"If you say so."

"Well, all I can say is . . . can I have peach cobbler for desert?"

"You're terrible."

"You raised me," Nathan quipped.

His words reminded of a task I wasn't looking forward to. In three years, he'd be eighteen, and I'd have to tell him that I wasn't his biological mother—but his aunt. Although I'd raised him, I didn't have a clue how he'd react to the information. My motives for not telling him had become fuzzy over the years, perhaps because I had changed.

Sometimes, not telling him felt like a big mistake. Other times, I felt I had done the right thing. He hadn't had to grow up wondering what his mother was like, and feeling shortchanged because she'd died and left him. He had been able to be my son because that's what he believed. I'd never once had to hear the ugly words, "You're not my mother!" Perhaps that was selfish of me. I don't know.

Thank God, Nathan didn't appear to be inheriting his mother's rebellious nature.

From the moment she was born, Sharene had given my parents nothing but grief. At least that's what they seemed to imply. Sharene was a teenager the night I was born. She threw a party while my dad was with my mother at the hospital, and she went through the entire liquor cabinet before a neighbor called the police. She had served four months in a juvenile detention home for that stunt.

A year later, she'd run away—coming back only when she found out she was pregnant. She'd gotten an abortion and had agreed to go back to school. Her high school years had been a nightmare for my parents. Drugs, reckless sex, detention, and breaking curfew were only a few of the horrors she put my parents through.

When I got old enough to witness the devastation she wreaked on my parents, I grew to hate her. Sharene hated me for a different reason. I was the angel she wasn't.

On the day Sharene graduated high school, she swiped my dad's ATM card, cleared out their small savings, and disappeared. I think my parents were too relieved to have her gone to file charges against her.

We didn't see her again for five years. One day, she just breezed in as if she hadn't been gone—not even bothering to hide the track marks on her arms. This was a thinner, harder Sharene. My parents greeted her warily, with understandable caution. They refused to leave me alone with her during the two weeks she stayed with us.

This time when she disappeared, she not only took Dad's credit card and car, but she robbed my piggy bank of the money I had been saving for my own phone line.

Dad reported his car stolen. They found it a week later, abandoned and stripped on a lonely country road a hundred miles from our town.

The next time we heard anything about Sharene was ten years later. A paramedic who'd arrived on the scene of her accident, found Dad's old credit card that he had long since canceled, and he had looked Dad's name up in the phone book.

I had cried at her funeral. I cried for my sister—who had shunned the love and support of her family. I'd never understood her, and now, I never would. But Sharene had left behind a part of herself that we could love.

Nathan.

"Mom? Are you okay? You look like you're about to cry."

I blinked and focused on Nathan. "I was just thinking of someone I knew a long time ago," I said.

At the Valentine's Day dance, Marvin ordered a soda at the bar.

He must have read the question in my eyes, because he laughed and said, "No, I'm not an alcoholic, although I was pretty wild in my younger days." He pulled out his keys and jiggled them in front of me. "I'm driving a beautiful woman home, tonight. Not only do I want to be clear-headed, but I want a fresh mouth when I kiss her good night." Gently, he reached out and closed my gaping mouth. "Have I told you how wonderful you look and smell tonight?"

Something very strange and bewildering happened then. My knees grew weak. I felt a strange, almost unfamiliar fluttering in my stomach, and it took me several moments to recognize the sensation.

It was desire.

I was attracted to Marvin.

The night was magical. I vaguely realized that Madison had come to the dance with someone else, but I didn't care. Marvin was not only a fabulous dancer, but he was a great conversationalist. He surprised me by totally avoiding any mention of his ex-wife, much to my relief. When I tried to tempt him just to see if he still had hang-ups about her, he set me straight right off the bat.

We were alone at our table. Tuesdai and her date were on the dance floor, laughing and dancing.

"So . . . how long were you married?"

Marvin grabbed my hand and began to trace teasing circles against my palm with his thumb. Little electric sensations began dancing along my arm, making it hard for me to concentrate.

"Eight years. One kid—a boy. She left me for my son's soccer coach." He looked earnest as he tugged me closer so that I could hear him over the band. "I really don't want to talk about her, okay? I love my son, and I miss him. Yes, I was heartbroken at first, but I'm over her."

"Okay." I felt a little embarrassed, but inwardly relieved. "How old is your son? Mine is fifteen. His name is Nathan."

His worried frown disappeared. "Eleven. His name is Patrick." With obvious pride, he reached for his wallet. I grabbed my purse and suddenly, we were laughing and grappling to see who could get their picture on the table first. Naturally, it was easier for Marvin, since he didn't have to wade through six months worth of receipts to find his wallet.

"Ta-da!" he announced, triumphantly. I gave him the picture of Nathan in his hockey uniform and took the picture Marvin held out. We were both silent for a moment as we studied our children.

I could definitely see Patrick's resemblance to Marvin in the brown eyes and dark hair. In fact, I also noticed the dimple showing in Patrick's right cheek, and I looked up to stare at that same dimple in Marvin's right cheek.

Slowly, my heart began to pound harder. I felt a strange shiver travel down my spine. My mother would have said a ghost had walked over my grave. Something tugged at my mind, something that stayed just out of reach.

Marvin tapped the picture of Nathan and laughed out loud, and the teasing memory was gone before I could fully grasp it.

"He looks like a pistol, all right."

I grinned. "That he is, but he's a good kid."

"With a mom like you, how could he be anything else?" Marvin looked at me, holding my gaze with a burning intensity that told me without words that this wasn't a meaningless flirtation for him. He meant business. "I can't wait to meet him."

Nathan would like Marvin, I realized with a tiny start of alarm. Things were moving too fast. Three days ago, I believed I was falling in love with someone else, and here I was fantasizing about Marvin meeting Nathan and the three of us becoming one happy little family.

"It's okay," Marvin said, reaching out to squeeze my hand. "I'm a very patient man, and it's obvious you've been hurt."

"It is?" I blurted out, blushing. I stared at my melting frozen daiquiri, sensing Marvin's curiosity.

"Um, he was married, and I didn't know it." To my relief and admiration, Marvin didn't push to hear more.

"Well, if you want to see my divorce papers, they're in the glove box of my car."

I sensed rather than saw his teasing smile, and I couldn't resist smiling back at him. "I believe you, but thanks for offering."

"Hey, don't take this the wrong way, but do you want to get out of here? I want to know all about you, and we can barely converse over this music."

Since I had been thinking the same thing, I jumped at his invitation. Just as we rose to leave, I felt a hand on my shoulder. I turned to find myself staring into Madison's handsome, smiling face.

His eyes were glittering, and I quickly realized he was drunk. As he swayed, his grip became bruising as he used me to support himself. Marvin must have heard me gasp, because he took Madison's hand from my shoulder, and he transferred it to the chair I had vacated. He kept his tone pleasant, but with a hint of censure.

"We were just about to leave, Madison. Having a good time?"

Madison looked from me to Marvin, then back to me again. "I wash . . . was just about to ask Brenna to dance."

Wondering how I could have once found him so attractive, I moved into the shelter of Marvin's arms before I said, "Sorry, Madison. Maybe some other time."

But instead of moving on, Madison's gaze narrowed on my flushed face. "Don't think I haven't notished . . . noticed the way you've been looking at me."

Hoping the dim lighting hid my scalding cheeks, I said, "I don't know what you're talking about. Let's go, Marvin."

Marvin practically shoved Madison out of the way without trying as we headed for the door.

I caught Tuesdai's eyes on the dance floor, and I waved at her. She grinned and winked at me before waving back. There was definite approval in her expression.

We found an all-night diner, and we settled into a booth, ordering coffee. We couldn't take our eyes off each other. If it wasn't love, it was something else equally as powerful.

"I want to hear everything about you," Marvin whispered. "Start from the beginning."

I did, omitting the part about Nathan not being my child, of course, but I did tell him a little about Sharene. "It was sad, not seeing her for years and then having to look at her serene, beautiful face in her coffin."

To my surprise, I found myself blinking back tears. I hadn't cried over Sharene in years.

"It sounds as if she would have had all the love and support she needed. It wasn't your fault, or your parents' fault, Brenna, that she didn't take advantage of it."

"I know." I sighed, wishing for once that I could confide in someone about Nathan—the gift Sharene had left us in the end. It was a secret I was weary of carrying around, I realized. Maybe Marvin would be the one I could eventually talk to about it.

"I dated a girl named Sharene once, back in my wild days. She was pretty wild, too." He huffed a laugh. "She was older than me, and I was just naive enough to think I was in love with her."

Again that odd shiver swept over me. I shuddered, drawing my arms together for warmth against the sudden chill. My heart began that maddening, slow pounding, again. "What . . . what was her last name?"

With a rueful smile, he shook his head. "She wouldn't tell me. Said she didn't want my parents coming after her for robbing the cradle. I was barely twenty. She was in her late twenties."

My mouth went dry. "She must have made a big impression on you."

"A guy never forgets his first love."

"How long ago was it?" I found myself holding my breath, and not knowing why. That eerie, nagging feeling was back. I felt on the verge of a huge discovery.

"I don't know . . . fifteen, sixteen years?"

The breath caught and held in my lungs until it began to burn. I let it out slowly. "Did she . . . did she call you 'Marv'?"

Marvin frowned. "As a matter of fact, she did. But how could you know that?"

The laugh that popped out of me was definitely hysterical. "This is . . . I can't . . ." Abruptly, I swung my knees around into the aisle so that I could put my head between them.

"Brenna? My God, are you okay? Is there something I can do? Are you sick?"

I managed a feeble wave as I waited for the encroaching blackness to fade from my vision. The air I sucked into my lungs felt like water, or syrup. The hard pounding of my heart had tripled, until I feared it would thump right up my throat and onto the floor.

The dimple in Marvin's right cheek . . . so like his son's—who also looked like Nathan. I had seen it, noticed it, but the implications had been too far-fetched for me to even consider.

Until Marvin told me about an old girlfriend named Sharene—who had called him Marv.

Even now I thought the odds were too incredible to be true. I had to be mistaken, delusional, or it was all just a fantastic coincidence.

When I was fairly certain I wasn't going to pass out and crack my head on the concrete floor, I lifted my head and carefully turned back around in the booth seat to face a very concerned Marvin.

My voice was raspy as I asked him, "Would you recognize Sharene if you saw her picture?"

Looking bewildered, he nodded. "I don't know how I could forget her. Like I said, she was my first love."

My fingers felt like ice as I pulled my purse onto my lap and found my billfold where I kept an old senior picture of Sharene. I took it out and stared into her defiant, go-to-hell expression before passing it across the table to Marvin.

He let out a shocked gasp. His wide-eyed gaze flickered to me, then back to the picture, then back to me, growing wider by the second. "This is Sharene. She's your sister?"

"Yes."

"How frigging amazing is that?" he said, his voice filled with awe.

He doesn't know the half of it, I thought, carefully choosing my words. I felt a moment's resentment that my sister had managed to come back from the grave to shadow my budding romance before I willed that resentment into silence.

When the shock wore off, I knew that I would be able to see a bright side to my amazing discovery. But right now, I was about to make Marvin a father.

"It . . . why are you looking at me like that?" Marvin asked, warily. "What happened between your sister and myself happened a long time ago."

"I know."

I took the picture and set it in the middle of the table. Sharene was going to be a part of this conversation, I decided. She was a part of it—just as she was a part of Nathan.

"If it wasn't for the dimple and the obvious resemblance, I'd say no way could this be true."

Marvin was beginning to show his frustration. He ran a hand through his hair, then he clasped his hands before him on the table. "Could you fill me in? Obviously, you know something I don't."

"It's going to be a shock," I warned. When Marvin didn't flinch, I continued as gently as I could. "Nathan isn't my son. Nobody knows that but my parents and me, and my parents are dead. He belonged to Sharene." Marvin continued to look at me blankly, not making the connection. "We didn't even know Sharene was pregnant when the paramedic called to tell us she was dead and they had preformed an emergency caesarean to save the baby. The only clue we could find out about the father was that she had been seeing someone she called Marv."

Marvin gasped. The color drained from his face, then came rushing back even brighter. His eyes looked huge as the full realization hit him. "You're saying that Nathan is my son? That's crazy!"

When I simply folded my arms and waited, he started shaking his head. Then he stared at me again, and his eyes dilated with shock.

"He is?" he asked, faintly.

I nodded. "I think so. I can't be sure, of course, but he does look like you and your son, and the timing is right. You . . . you don't have to do anything about it, Marvin. I'm Nathan's mother. I've raised him on my own, and he never has to know about you."

I meant it, too. Marvin had been very young at the time, seduced by a woman in her late twenties. While some might say that Marvin had been a man who knew his own mind, I found the age difference more than a little sickening. He'd been a few years older than my Nathan was now.

"This is wild . . . insane!" He ran a hand through his hair again, making it stand on end and giving him a harassed appearance.

No wonder, I thought. I had dropped a whopper of a bomb onto him.

Before I knew it, the words popped out of my mouth, "Maybe I shouldn't have told you."

"No!"

His vehement reaction really startled and shocked me.

"If I'm Nathan's father, then I want him to know, and I want to be a part of his life. Yes, I'm shocked. Stupefied would be a more accurate description, but I'm getting over it. I'm sure you're just as shocked."

I managed a faint smile. "That would be an understatement. My date turned out to be my son's father. Sounds like a soap opera script to me."

"I . . . I want to meet him," Marvin said, sounding steadier. "Could I? I won't say anything until you're ready," he rushed on to assure me.

I'd be lying if I said I didn't feel a little jealousy at the thought of sharing Nathan with Marvin, and of sharing Marvin with Nathan. It was confusing to say the least. In the end I said the only thing I could say.

"Sure, you can meet him. If, um, you want, we can get a DNA test done so you'd know for certain."

"What a night," he said, putting some money on the table for the coffee. The smile he flashed at me was very close to normal.

"Found the girl of my dreams and a son I didn't know I had—all in one night."

Nathan was in the den watching television when Marvin and I came into the house. I don't know who was more nervous—Marvin or me—as I introduced them and waited for Nathan's reaction. I knew my son, and I knew that he was quick to judge, but also perceptive.

He gave Marvin a thorough dustup as he clasped his hand in a manly handshake. I could tell by the slightly pained expression on Marvin's face and the grin, that Nathan was trying to squeeze the life out of him.

It was a man thing, Nathan had told me once.

125

"Hey, Mr. Addison. Nice to meet you."

Marvin feigned horror. "No! Please, call me Marvin. Mr. Addison makes me feel like I'm an old man."

"But, you are—"

I goosed Nathan, and he made a big show of losing his breath before a big grin split his freckled face. I let out a silent sigh of relief. Nathan approved, and he was proving it by goofing around with Marvin.

They talked for a bit about hockey and soccer, then Nathan shot me an exaggerated wink before announcing he was going to bed. Upstairs. Behind closed doors where he couldn't hear a thing.

Blushing furiously, I finally had to push him in that direction before he mortified me beyond recovery.

"Would you like a glass of wine or something?" I asked, nervous now that we were alone again and he'd met his son. I didn't want to be selfish, but I wanted to recapture the romantic atmosphere we'd been caught up in before I found out he was very likely Nathan's father—if that were possible.

I knew I'd be disappointed if it wasn't.

"Water would be great," Marvin said.

I was very conscious of his intense gaze following me to the refrigerator as I brought out a bottle of spring water and some white wine for myself. Right then, I needed a drink in the worst way.

Handing him the water, I poured myself a glass of wine and took a drink. The moment the glass left my lips, Marvin said, "Wait!" He nearly startled me into dropping it.

I stared at him, frozen. He reached out and took the glass from my lifeless fingers, his gaze on my mouth. "Don't lick your lips," he whispered, huskily. "I want to do it."

My breath caught and held as he slowly bent his mouth to mine. He softly swept his tongue over my lips, then he angled his mouth over mine. It was the sweetest, yet hottest kiss I could ever remember getting. By the time he lifted his head, I was ready to collapse into a helpless puddle in the kitchen floor.

"Wow," I said, making him chuckle.

"Yeah, wow!" He touched his forehead to mine, looking deeply into my eyes. He was smiling. "Thank-you for the most incredible night of my life."

I grinned. "Don't you mean the most shocking?"

He shook his head. "Uh-uh. I mean the most incredible. I think I'm falling in love with you, Brenna."

My brow shot upward, but inside I was melting like a hot candle. "After one date? Was it something I said?"

We both laughed at that, then he kissed me again… and again.

Marvin and I got married six months later. On the eve of our wedding, we sat down with an ecstatic Nathan and told him the entire story, assuring him that if he didn't approve, we would postpone our wedding until after his graduation.

Nathan was understandably stunned, but after a brief moment of shock as he absorbed our incredible news, he nearly brought the house down with his excited shouts. He admitted he was pretty bummed to find out I wasn't his real mother, but then decided in the next breath that the biological part didn't really count, since I had raised him from birth.

As for Marvin turning out to be his father, Nathan couldn't believe his great fortune!

The End

A SEASON OF LOVE OR HATE?
Racial Prejudice Nearly Lost Us Our
Dream Home– But We Wouldn't Let It!

I was planning to marry the man of my dreams on Valentine's Day—the perfect day for lovers. But my fiancé and I experienced the opposite of love when we tried buying a house.

I suppose it shouldn't have come as a surprise. Michael and I had been a classic case of "love at first sight," when we'd met at the home of mutual friends.

But when Michael got down on one knee right there in the grass at our neighborhood park, I was stunned. Before I could gather my thoughts, he had pulled a ring from his pocket. It shimmered in the light of the setting sun.

"Lauren, you have brought such joy into my life. I can't imagine living the rest of it without you. Will you marry me?"

There'd been no need for me to think. My answer came instantly.

"Yes . . . Yes, yes!"

He smiled as he slipped the ring on my finger. Then, we were in each other's arms, and he was kissing me, and life was oh, so good.

At some point, we sat back down on the park bench.

"You certainly surprised me," I said.

His smile, as always, caused my heart to flutter.

"You knew it was only a matter of time. I've loved you from the first minute I laid eyes on you."

I nodded, remembering the night. My best friend, Betsy, had told me about this great guy her hubby worked with. I'd told her not to start matchmaking as I'd had it with guys. I was tired of them trying to get me in bed after the first date. But she told me this guy was different.

"What are you thinking?" he asked.

"About that night."

"The night I fell in love with you," he added.

"It was the same for me. I had no intention of getting caught up in Betsy's little matchmaking scheme. Then, you walked in, and I couldn't take my eyes off you. Of course, none of the women could."

He laughed that laugh I loved to hear, laughter that warmed me inside and made me smile.

"You're exaggerating," he said.

I shook my head.

"Come on, now; you know your dark good looks turn women's heads all the time."

"I wouldn't know. I only have eyes for you, my darling, Lauren. For now and always."

"You say the nicest things, Michael."

Then, we settled back to watch the last golden rays of the setting sun.

"This is such a lovely time of day," I said, snuggling up against him. "And I love sharing sunsets in the park with you."

"Me too," he said. "That's why I wanted to propose right here where we've had so many special times."

"It was the perfect place, and the ring is absolutely the most beautiful I have ever seen."

"Beautiful ring for a beautiful woman."

Our lips met again, and his kiss held the promise of happily ever after.

We sat for a while longer before I thought about my parents. I suddenly wanted to share our joy with them.

"Can we go and tell my parents?" I asked.

Laughter again as he took me in his arms.

"You look like a little girl who can't wait to tell a secret!"

"You're right. I can't wait to tell them. They already love you, and this news is going to make them so happy."

"Why do you say they love me?" he asked.

"Because they do. You're good to me. They've seen me hurt all too often by other men and appreciate you for the loving, caring gentle man you are. Now, let's go tell them."

We talked all the way to my parents' home—about the kind of wedding we'd like, about having babies, and buying a big house to raise a family in.

As we talked about the kind of house we wanted, Michael grew quiet.

"What's wrong?" I asked.

Another moment of silence, then he spoke softly.

"Growing up, our house was so small, babe. My two brothers and I slept in one bed. I don't ever want our kids to have to sleep in the same bed."

He got real quiet again, like he always did when he talked about his childhood.

I knew he was thinking about his two brothers who didn't make it out of the old neighborhood alive.

I reached over and squeezed his arm.

"Michael, you have a terrific job, and with the bonus you got on your last promotion, I don't think you ever have to worry about our kids sleeping in the same bed. Plus, we also have my salary."

"But you're going to quit working when we have kids, right? We're agreed on that?"

"You bet. I'll be a stay-at-home mom. You make enough money to support a family quite nicely."

For several moments, he seemed lost in thought, again.

"Hey, where'd you go this time?" I asked.

He sighed.

"Back to Pennsylvania. But just for a minute. I was thinking of my dad. Wishing he were still alive so he could get to know you. I'm also wishing I could thank him again for moving me and mom here, near her sisters after my brother, Johnny's, death. My mom barely managed to get through losing two of her sons. I remember Dad holding me close right after my second brother's funeral. 'We can't lose you, Michael,'" he said. 'It would kill your mother.'"

"Then, he cried. My father cried like a baby. I remember the tears dripping down onto my cheeks."

He took a deep breath, struggling to put that memory aside.

Then, he turned to me and smiled.

"I am also thankful that we moved here because if we hadn't, I would never have met you and would have died a lonely old man."

It was my turn to smile.

"I doubt you would have died lonely."

"Yes, I would have. Because you are my soul mate, made just for me. You're the only woman I could find happiness with. If we'd stayed in Pennsylvania, I would never have married, wandering the earth in search of the other half of my heart."

He often said such lovely, endearing things, and it added to the warm feeling I felt deep inside when we were together. "In that case, I, too, am sorry I can't thank your father. Because if you'd stayed in Pennsylvania, I would have died a lonely old woman—never finding the one man made for me. And believe me, my love, when we met, I was ready to swear off men— thinking they were all interested in only one thing."

"We are," he said, trying not to laugh.

I smacked his arm, playfully.

"Well, at least you didn't try to get me in bed after our first date."

"It's not that I didn't want to," he said, unable to stop the laughter this time.

I had to smile.

"But you waited. For that, I love you even more."

We pulled into my parents' driveway, and I saw the porch light come on.

"Let's go," I said, getting out of the car. "This is going to be such fun."

And it was. Mom and Dad were almost as happy as me. They welcomed Michael into the family, hugging us both at the same time.

Then, Dad went and got out a bottle of wine to celebrate with a toast.

After we'd all settled down a bit, Mom took my hand in hers.

"Lauren, I've been waiting for this day a long time. When do you think you'll get married?"

The thought came to me in an instant, even though I'd not thought of a date before. "Valentine's Day," I said. "The perfect day for a wedding."

"You're right," Mom answered. "It is the perfect day, so romantic."

I turned to my future husband.

"How do you feel about that date?"

"Not so good. It's more than six months away. I'm not sure I can wait that long."

"Oh, Michael," Mom said, "It's going to be hard enough to plan a wedding in just six months. Some places are booked up a year or more in advance."

"Now, Mom," I cautioned, "we don't want a huge wedding . . . do we, Michael?"

"At this point," he said, "I defer to the women in the family, just as I do in my own."

Michael's mother and two aunts were all the family he had left now, and he treated them with deep respect and much love. It was another of his good qualities.

Suddenly, Mom started talking in earnest about the wedding.

"We can have a heart-shaped wedding cake, Lauren. Wouldn't that be lovely and romantic?"

I had to smile.

"Yes, it would, Mom."

"In fact," she continued, "let's plan the whole wedding around the holiday . . . we'll have pink and red flowers, and your bridesmaids' dresses can be pink or red, too. Napkins, plates . . . everything will go along with the Valentine's Day theme. It's always been a day filled with love, and it will be a wonderful day to get married.

"Oh, and the wedding will be in our church . . . right?" Mom asked, a bit haltingly. That's when Dad jumped in. "Rosemarie, give the kids time to enjoy their engagement, for gosh sakes. Michael will be wishing he'd eloped if you don't slow down."

"Eloping sounds like a grand idea. No need to wait six months, then," Michael said, with a grin.

Mom looked stricken.

"Oh, no. I want my only daughter to have a wedding, Michael. I've dreamt about this day for years. The only reason I brought up the church is simply because we've never discussed your religion. I wasn't sure if you'd have an objection to getting married in our church."

"I'm a Christian, Mrs. Anderson. I'll marry Lauren anywhere she wants to be married."

So the church issue was settled, and Mom moved on to a place for the reception. Once again, Dad stepped in.

"Okay, we are going to let these two love birds go now, so they can celebrate their engagement," he said. "You women can talk about the details another day." Dad turned back to us, taking my hand in his. "We do thank you both for coming to tell us. We appreciate that."

"Oh, yes," Mom said, giving me a hug. "It was so thoughtful of you to share your news right away, sweetie. And Dad's right, we can talk about the details some other time."

Minutes later, we were driving away.

"Hope my mom didn't scare you with all that talk about the wedding. And really . . . if you'd rather just elope, I'm fine with that."

He reached over and took my hand in his.

"No way. We could not do that to your mother, nor mine. A wedding is a special time for them too. Let's allow them to enjoy every minute."

I leaned against him, my head on his shoulder, despite the seat belt's restriction.

"I love you so much."

"And I love you. More than you can ever know," he answered.

The next few months were filled with wedding plans. After finding the perfect place for the reception, we had to go to Mom's favorite bakery and taste cakes, then we went on a search for a photographer and a florist. Michael never complained.

"As long as it all ends in our marriage, nothing else matters," he told me.

The holidays were special family times that year, as Michael's family came to my parents' home for Thanksgiving and we all went to his mom's for Christmas.

Once the holidays were past, Valentine's Day seemed very close.

I had to admit, all the hearts and flowers touches my mother came up with would add much to our celebration. Once all the plans were finalized, Michael and I set out in earnest to find the home of our dreams.

We'd been looking for months. Even during the holidays, we drove through many of the surrounding small towns, looking for a place we could call our own. We saw a couple that came close to what we were looking for, but none of them had all the items we wanted—a big house with at least four bedrooms and a large kitchen meant for cooking and eating in. We also wanted a nice sized yard with lots of shade trees, and it had to be near a good school district. We planned to start a family as soon as possible, and we wanted our children to grow up in a good neighborhood and get the best education possible.

Michael had worked hard after his dad's death and put himself through school. He learned everything there was to know about computers. The company he worked for installed and maintained computer systems in offices, banks, and malls. Michael went in and figured out exactly what they needed, ordered the systems, and did anything that needed done to keep them operating efficiently.

In addition to Michael's salary, I made a good living as an E.R. nurse.

We could—thank God—afford a nice home.

Shortly after welcoming in the new year with love and much hope for our future, we were driving through a rather new, small housing development about twenty minutes from my parents' home. There were only eleven houses in the plan, each unique and lovely, set on a half acre of gently sloped land with lots of shade trees. And the best part of all: one of the homes had a "For Sale by Owner" sign in front of it.

"Lauren, this is perfect. Look at the trees, and all that space between the homes. Can you read the phone number?"

"Yes, I've got it," I said, jotting the number in my notebook.

Michael looked at me and smiled.

"I think we just got lucky."

The next day, I called the number from work, but got an answering machine. There was a message that if the call was regarding the house, the inside could be seen via photos on the Internet. I took down the website, and after checking it out, got even more excited. It was better than what we'd imagined. I called Michael, and he said he'd check it out, too.

When he called back, the excitement in his voice matched my own.

"You're right. It's terrific and only a year old. Usually, in a year, all the kinks in a new place are worked out. But it's not old enough to need anything updated. You want to go see it, right?"

"Of course, as soon as we can."

"Listen," he said. "I'm going to be late for my meeting if I don't hustle. Would you mind calling and making an appointment for tonight, if possible—but early enough to see it in the daylight."

"Mind?... not at all, honey. I can't wait to see it. I really do think this is the one. What time can you pick me up?"

"If I get out on time, I can be there around five. We should make it over there before dark. Leave a message on my machine, or e-mail me if there's any change."

"Okay. Good luck at your meeting."

"Thanks, babe. Love you."

"Love you, too."

As soon as I hung up, I tried the phone number again, and this time, a woman answered. I told her that my fiancé and I were interested in the house and asked the price, breathing a sigh of relief when the figure she quoted was in our price range.

"Can we make an appointment to see it as soon as possible?" I asked. "We're getting married on Valentine's Day, and we're hoping to find a house before the wedding."

Mrs. Marshall congratulated me; then, she said if it was convenient for us, we could come anytime after five.

"That would be great. In fact, if I can get my fiance to leave work earlier, could we come around five? That would give us a bit more daylight to see the outside."

"Five is fine," Mrs. Marshall said. "What is your name, again?"

"Lauren . . . Lauren Anderson. My fiancé's name is Michael Talbot."

"Okay, Lauren, see you at five."

I immediately dialed Michael's number. When the answering machine beeped, I left a message asking if he could get out a half hour earlier.

I left work, hurrying back to my apartment—anxious to change clothes and head out to see the house. I felt like a little kid waiting for Christmas.

The phone rang a few minutes after four.

"Hi babe, sorry it's not going to work out for tonight," Michael said. "We have a major problem with a computer system we installed for an insurance company. They're located almost an hour away at the opposite end of town. Even if I figure out the problem, there's no way I could make it, tonight."

"Oh, honey, I'm so sorry you have to work late. But I'm even sorrier about canceling this appointment. I'm so anxious to see the house."

"Lauren, there's no reason for you to cancel. We both know it's exactly what we've been looking for. Find out why they're selling—in a diplomatic way, of course. If the inside is as nice as the outside—and it sure appeared to be from what was posted on the Internet—just make them an offer. Ask if they'd consider five thousand less than their asking price. That would help us pay for closing costs, at least."

"Are you sure you want me to do this without you?" I asked.

"You know we've been looking for months, and this is the first house that has everything we want. I'd hate to see someone call tomorrow and buy it right out from under us."

"Okay, you talked me into it. Will you have your cell phone on in case I have a question?"

"Sure, no problem. I'll keep the phone on. Oh, and you better take a check along. If you like the house and make an offer, they might just accept. Then, it would be a good idea to put hand money down to hold it."

"Okay, will do. I better get moving or I'll be late."

"Bye babe. Love you . . . and good luck."

"Love you too, but I wish you were going with me."

"Me too. Bye."

That evening, Mrs. Marshall greeted me warmly. I explained why Michael couldn't be there, and then, we started looking at the property. I didn't have to ask why they were selling. She offered the information as soon as we started looking at the back yard.

"I'm going to hate to leave here," she said, with obvious regret in her voice. "We've lived here almost a year and love the area. Our kids love the school. Our neighbors are great. We're minutes from grocery stores, and a mall is fifteen minutes away. It's like living in the country with all the conveniences of city living." She sighed, then continued. "My husband's company is moving to California and made him an offer he just couldn't refuse. I'm just hoping we can find a comparable house, there."

"I hope so, too," I said.

"Well, as you can see the patio is fieldstone. My husband and I designed it, along with the stone wall with the built in barbeque grill." She glanced around. "These trees shade the whole back yard in the summer, Lauren. It's a wonderful place for kids to play."

"That's one reason we liked this location," I said. "We hope to have a big family."

She smiled.

"We have three, and are sort of planning for one more. Kids are such fun. "Would you like to see the inside, now?"

By the time I'd seen the first floor master bedroom and bath, I knew this was the house Michael and I would be living in. I felt at home as I walked through the rooms, imagining us in front of the fireplace in the winter, or on the patio in the summer. It was like a dream come true. The kitchen was exactly what I'd hoped for with a center island and a window above the sink, overlooking the lovely yard. I could imagine the trees in the summer and in the fall. I could even imagine how it would look after a snowfall.

The second floor had three more bedrooms—enough for a nice size family.

When I'd seen the whole house and basement, Mrs. Marshall asked what I thought of it.

"I know most prospective buyers at this point would hem and haw a bit and say, we'll think about it, but I'm not most people, and I have to tell you I love the house. My fiance liked what he saw of it on the Internet, and told me to go ahead and make an offer. I know you'll have to run it past your husband, but as you can tell, I'm anxious to settle things before our wedding."

Her smile grew broader the longer I talked.

"Most homeowners, at this point, would have to say we'll think about it, too. But since Bill has to be in the new office in three weeks, we would love to have this settled so I don't have to do all the packing myself after he leaves. What's your offer?"

I told her what Michael had suggested. "Do you think that's reasonable?" I asked.

She smiled, again.

"Isn't it funny?" she said. "You know everyone goes a bit higher than what they really want for the house, knowing the buyer is going to try and get it for less. Would you have a seat while I call my husband. I'll see what he says."

She went back into the kitchen, while I sat in the spacious living room—already dreaming of our life here in this house.

Mrs. Marshall came back in with a smile on her face.

"My husband says we accept."

"Oh, I'm so glad."

"I think this was meant to be," she said. "It's perfect timing for us with the move coming up in a few weeks, and if we can get the bank to move quickly on the closing, you'll have time to get the house ready to move into before your wedding."

My mind was whirling. The wedding and a new house. But she was right. It was perfect timing.

"Okay . . . this is great. Oh, when you talk to your bank, you might let them know that we've been pre-approved by our bank for a loan that will cover the price we've agreed on."

"Great," she said. "That should really move things along quickly."

"And," I went on, "I brought a check to put hand money down to hold the house till everything goes through. My phone number is on it if you have to reach us for any reason." I took a deep breath. "Can't believe we've finally found the home we've been dreaming of!"

"I know you'll love it here, Lauren."

"I think so, too," I said. "Now, is there anything else we need to know, or do before the closing?"

"Actually there is one more thing. No big deal. This development has a homeowner's association. It was formed by all of us to protect our property values. As you pointed out, the grounds—which include our backyards—are quite nice, and we wanted them to stay that way. We drew up what they call a restrictive covenant, outlining what we homeowners can and can't do."

"I've heard of that. My mother's friend bought a house in Florida, and they had to get approval before painting their house, and something about the type of mailbox they put up. Is it something like that?"

"Exactly. We all vote on a variety of things, like no trailers or boats parked in the driveways. You can plant shrubbery, but must keep it below six feet in height. You can't put up a flagpole. Stuff like that. It keeps our little neighborhood looking nice."

"Sounds fine with me."

"In fact, there's a meeting next Sunday. It might be nice for you to come and meet your new neighbors."

"That would be great," I said.

We talked as I wrote out the check, and she gave me a receipt. Mrs. Marshall—Karen—as she told me to call her—and I talked easily. I almost felt bad that she wouldn't be living there. She would have been a nice neighbor.

"Okay," she said as we finished up. "You give me a call when your fiance is able to come see the house, and I should have the information on the closing by then. If there's any paperwork that needs to be done before that, I'll give you a call."

Michael was thrilled that the house was going to be ours. He couldn't wait to see it, so I called the next day to ask Karen if I could bring him out that evening. She agreed.

When we pulled into the driveway, Michael was grinning from ear to ear.

"It's so perfect. I can't believe it. Wait till my mom sees it!"

"We'll have lots of fun family times, here," I said.

We rang the bell, and when Karen opened the door, she had a smile on her face. I saw her eyes as she glanced behind me. It was a look I'd seen before. Women were taken with Michael's good looks. Then, I saw something else. I'd seen that look before too, on our first date. I still remembered it. We'd gone to dinner, and I couldn't believe the way people stared at us.

I'd been able to see beyond Michael's color within a few minutes of meeting him. But people who didn't know him . . . saw only a white woman with a black man.

Michael's voice broke into the awkward silence.

"Hi. You must be Karen. I'm Lauren's fiance, Michael." He extended his hand, and Karen shook it. Before she had a chance to say anything, Michael spoke.

"Karen, you have a fantastic home. You and your husband have obviously put much love and attention into every detail." He glanced into the living room. "I've seen the house on your website, and the furnishings are incredible. Did you have a decorator?"

"Oh, no. We did everything ourselves."

With that, we were on our way as she proudly showed us through the house.

I had to smile. Michael had done exactly what he'd done with my parents and others he meets for the first time. He talks about something they care about, compliments them, ask questions, and listens. Within minutes, I had no doubt Karen had already looked beyond his color. Of course, being so easy to look at probably didn't hurt, either. Michael was just plain gorgeous.

"Can't thank you enough for letting us spend so much time looking at the house and property, Karen," Michael said, as we got ready to leave. "I can see it's not going to be easy for you to leave here. It's obvious that you love the place."

She nodded.

"We do. As I told Lauren, the kids love it here, our neighbors are all nice people, and the house is great."

"Too bad the kids aren't here," Michael said. "We would have liked to meet them and your husband, too."

"Actually, the kids are anxious to meet whoever is going to be living in their house," she said with a smile. "Maybe when you come to the homeowner's association meeting, you can stop in and meet them."

"That would be great," I said, pleased that Karen wanted us to meet her children.

"As for Bill," she continued, "he's busy trying to find us a house in California."

"It won't be easy coming up with something comparable to what you have here," Michael said.

Karen sighed.

"That's what my husband is concerned about, but he's hopeful."

"Well, thanks again for the tour," I said, as we walked toward the entry.

"Yes, it was a pleasure seeing your home and knowing how happy you and your family have been here," Michael added.

"It was a pleasure talking to both of you, too," Karen said as she opened the front door. "Now don't forget, the homeowner's association is meeting on Sunday afternoon at three. It's at Ray & Gladys Chapman's house." She pointed down the street. "It's that buff brick, two-story house right at the end of the cul-de-sac."

"Okay, we'll see you there, Sunday at three," Michael said. "And thanks again."

As we walked to the car, I squeezed Michael's hand.

"What do you think?"

"The house is perfect," he said. "The best part is that Karen Marshall didn't try canceling the deal when she saw me at the door."

"Oh, Michael, they couldn't do that, could they? I put money down on it."

"Lauren, you have not lived in my shoes . . . or I should say, my skin? People do lots of things they couldn't or shouldn't do because of my skin color."

"We've talked about this, Michael. I still don't understand how anyone can judge you by the color of your skin."

"And I've told you before, they're not just judging me. They're wondering why you are with me. You're being judged, too."

I shook my head.

"Well, I don't like it."

"I don't, either." He sighed deeply; then he said, "Let's change the subject, and talk about our new home. I can hardly wait to move in with my wife."

The next few days flew by with lots of last-minute wedding stuff to do. Another weekend came, and once again, Michael and I attended Sunday services with my parents. He'd started going with us right after our engagement—wanting to be a part of the church even before our wedding. There had been some whispering that first Sunday— which upset me, but Mom told me to ignore it.

"You love Michael," she said, "and eventually everyone who knows and loves you will accept him, too."

"But Mom, these are supposedly Christian people. They shouldn't be talking about us in church!"

"No, they shouldn't, but it's human nature, I suppose. They'll get past it in time."

And they did. The more services and special events we attended during those next few months, the more friendly people became. I'd known most of the parishioners since I was a little girl, so eventually they accepted Michael just as Mom said they would.

That Sunday morning, we had breakfast with Mom and Dad after church. They were anxious to see the house, so I promised I'd ask the Marshalls if we could bring them by, soon.

"We'll take Michael's mom, too. I'm sure Karen will be okay with that. She's been so nice."

When we dropped my parents off after breakfast, Dad wished us good luck at the meeting. Before I had a chance to ask why we needed luck, he continued.

"Don't be surprised if some of the other homeowners aren't as . . . accepting of Michael as the owner of that house was."

"Dad!"

Michael put his hand on my arm.

"Lauren, I understand exactly what your father is saying. We have to be ready for some disapproval, there."

"They'll change when they get to know you."

Dad smiled.

"I'm sure they will," he said.

Michael was so quiet as we headed across town. I had to say something.

"Karen wants us to stop and see their children after the meeting."

Michael nodded.

"Do you realize that she wouldn't do that if she didn't like us, if she felt it was wrong for us to be together?"

"Like your dad said, Lauren, not everyone is going to feel that way."

"Well, we'll just have to win them over, one by one. I'll be extra nice, and you will have to be your most charming self."

That finally made Michael smile as he gave a mock salute.

"Yes, ma'am, I'll do my best, ma'am."

He made me laugh, and we approached Ray Chapman's house with smiles on our faces.

Only when we got to the front door did our smiles falter. The look on the man who opened the door was one of obvious disapproval.

"May I help you?" he asked, though it was plain to see he did not want to help us in any way.

"Yes. I'm Michael Talbot, and this is my fiancee, Lauren Anderson. We're buying the Marshall's house, and Karen invited us to the meeting so we could meet our new neighbors."

About midway through Michael's introduction, I saw Karen approaching the door from the rear of the room. She was smiling at us, but it was obvious to me that the smile was rather strained. I had a feeling she'd just told the members who their new neighbors were going to be.

"Hi, Lauren . . . Michael," she said. "This is Ray Chapman. He's president of the association."

Michael extended his hand.

"Nice to meet you, Ray."

I could tell it wasn't easy for that man to shake Michael's hand.

The chill in the room after we entered was enough to turn water into ice. Even as Karen introduced us—telling everyone that I was a nurse, and Michael was a computer systems analyst—I could see the disapproval in their eyes. Only Karen and one other woman spoke to us while we waited for the meeting to begin.

They opened the meeting, and started discussing the first item on the agenda, which dealt with a raise in taxes. It was a heated discussion. They eventually went on to the second item on the agenda, which dealt with a change in the lawn service company. I tried to relax, despite the uncomfortable feeling I had sitting in a room full of people who so obviously disapproved of Michael and me.

Mom was right after all, and Dad and Michael, too. Maybe I'd been a fool to think people weren't as prejudiced as they had been years ago. All I could do was say a silent prayer that somehow, someway, we could change their opinion of us.

My parents had. Although even before they met him, they tried to warn me how difficult it would be if we married and had children.

"It's not going to be easy to deal with the way people treat you," Mom said.

Dad agreed.

"Why do you want to put yourself through this, Lauren?" he'd asked.

"Because he's the kindest, sweetest man I've ever met. He's a man who takes care of his mother, a man who loves children. He's a man I can trust, and the only man I've met in the last few years that hasn't tried to get me in bed after the first date."

My words had shocked Dad, but also made him realize the kind of man Michael was. They agreed to meet him, and though a bit uncomfortable at first, Michael quickly won them over. Though fond of him, they were still concerned about me. In the end, they'd accepted my decision to marry him because he was a good man who treated me right. That's what most parents want for their daughters.

Ray Chapman's voice abruptly cut into my thoughts.

"Is there anyone who has anything to add to the agenda?"

I raised my hand, and Michael moved to stop me, then let me go.

"Yes? . . . it's Lauren, right?" Ray asked.

"Yes, my name's Lauren Anderson," I said as I stood. "My fiance, Michael and I, are buying Karen and Bill Marshall's home."

Mr. Chapman cleared his throat.

"Lauren, I hope Karen informed you that the association's members have to approve a buyer before the closing."

I couldn't believe my ears.

This could not be happening.

I glanced down at Karen who looked very uncomfortable.

"Karen told me there was a restrictive covenant, and we went over many of the things it covers—like the height of bushes and no flagpoles. She did not tell me that you all have to approve us before we close on the house. And I have a feeling that if I asked you for a copy of the covenant right now, you would be hard-pressed to be able to point out that clause to me."

Ray Chapman grew decidedly red around the ears, and I knew if I wanted to make a stink, that I could bring up the illegality of them even attempting to keep us from buying the house because of Michael's race.

But I didn't have the stomach for a fight, not with people I hoped would be good neighbors, eventually. Michael evidently didn't, either. He stood up, and took my hand in his.

"As Lauren said, I'm Michael Talbot, her fiance. I'd like to say a few words. You don't know us, and we don't know any of you besides Karen. But I think we're all very much alike deep inside. Like all of you, we fell in love and want to get married and raise a family. When we saw your community, we loved it immediately. It's exactly the kind of place we want our children to grow up in.

"Karen and Bill's house is beautiful. We are as excited at the prospect of living there as each of you must have been when you bought your houses. Karen has told us that you are terrific neighbors, and I am hopeful that because you are good people, you will try and look past the fact that I'm not the same color you are."

People in the room were looking down at their shoes or shifting in their seats.

I couldn't stand it. I had to say something.

"Michael and I chose Valentine's Day for our marriage. I thought it was the perfect day for two people who love each other to get married. When we set out to find the perfect house to move into after the wedding, we were looking for a house big enough for the babies we pray God will send us... a house with lots of space around it... a house that has a warm and cheery kitchen where we would cook meals together, and have friends and family in to visit."

I paused, and when I noticed several of the women looking at me and continued. "We found the perfect house, the perfect neighorhood with lots of space for kids to play. When we met Karen, we talked easily, and she told me this was a good place to live. She told me the neighbors were great, and she would miss living here.

"As Michael said, we want exactly what all of you want from a home and a neighborhood. We want to be happy and content. We want to live in peace, and raise a family in a good community.

"I know you are all feeling a bit uncomfortable about us right now, just as my parents did when I first brought Michael home. But I'm willing to take Karen at her word. She said you are good people, good neighbors . . . so I know you'll give us a chance to show we are good people, too, and we will be good neighbors."

I was surprised when Karen stood up and asked to have the floor.

"Go ahead," Ray said.

"You all have only known me and my family for a year," she began, "but Bill and I have formed close friendships with many of you in that short time. This little community is like the old neighborhood I grew up in, where people cared about each other.

"I've spent time with Lauren and Michael. Lauren first came and shared her dreams for a home and family with me. And yes, when I met Michael, I was a bit taken aback, but by the end of that evening they spent in my home, I had no doubt that he and Lauren would be exactly the kind of neighbors you want to have. I just hope you will all be the kind of neighbors I told them you are."

There were several seconds of dead silence, then a man in the back of the room stood.

"Can I have the floor, Ray?"

"Go ahead, Jack," Ray Chapman said, obviously glad to have

somebody else take the floor. Michael, Karen, and I sat down.

"I'd like to make a motion that we welcome our newest neighbors, Lauren and Michael."

"I second that motion," said a woman up front.

There was a pause, but finally, Ray Chapman begrudgingly said, "All those in favor, say aye."

A chorus of "ayes" met his words.

"Opposed?"

No one said, "nay" so Ray banged his gavel on the table and said, "Motion carried."

He then closed the meeting.

People began to get up and one by one, came by and shook our hands, adding their own words of welcome.

Mrs. Chapman invited everyone to go into the dining room to have coffee and cookies.

I thanked Karen for standing up for us.

"I only spoke what I felt," she said. "I hope you'll be happy here— despite men like Ray and a couple others."

Jack, the man who made the motion on our behalf, was one of the last to speak to us. Michael shook his hand, and began to thank him.

Jack shook his head and interrupted.

"No need to say anything, young man. I expect a favor in return for my motion."

We both looked at him in surprise. "A favor?" Michael repeated.

He nodded, then turned to me. "Lauren, you have a lot of spunk. I'm going to count on you to tackle the county on that ridiculous tax assessment. I think you have just what it takes to get those commissioners to listen."

He and Michael were both looking at me but I couldn't think of a word to say.

"Well, Jack," Michael said, "you just did the impossible. You left my bride-to-be speechless."

The three of us ended up laughing. I could see Ray Chapman watching us.

He was scowling as he headed into the dining room without another word to us.

"Now Ray, there might be a tough nut to crack," Jack said. "Hope you two are up to the job."

I took Michael's hand in mine.

"Oh, we are Jack. We are!"

The End